Madrigal

A Novel

Marilyn Parkes-Seddon

A.H. STOCKWELL
PUBLISHERS SINCE 1898

Published in 2023 by
Marilyn Parkes-Seddon
in association with
Arthur H Stockwell Ltd
West Wing Studios
Unit 166, The Mall
Luton, Bedfordshire
ahstockwell.co.uk

British Library Cataloguing-in-Publication Data:
A catalogue record for this book is available from the British Library.
ISBN 9780722353059

To Samantha, my greatly loved sister

Contents

Acknowledgements

With heartfelt thanks to my friend Patricia Hall for typing and amending my manuscript and to her husband Peter Hall, who proof-read the manuscript as his wife typed.

With thanks also to my friend Margaret for her encouragement.

I cannot forget my husband Malc; I could not have done this without your support, encouragement and patience.

A special thanks to my much-loved niece Elisabeth for her hand-drawn map of Guernsey. This map is authentic, but I have used a little artistic licence with some places named in my novel.

About the Author

Originally from Wigan in Lancashire, Marilyn Parkes-Seddon gained an honours degree in Applied Social Science, and then a Master's degree in Social Policy, followed by an MBA.

Whilst working for a Social Services department for many years in Wigan, she had always had an ambition to write. Retirement on grounds of ill health gave her the opportunity to fulfil that ambition. Her first novel, *The Jonquil*, also set in the Channel Islands, was published in 2019. She now lives with her husband Malc in South West Scotland.

Previous publications:

The Jonquil
Seeking The Scallop Shell (non-fiction)

MADRIGAL

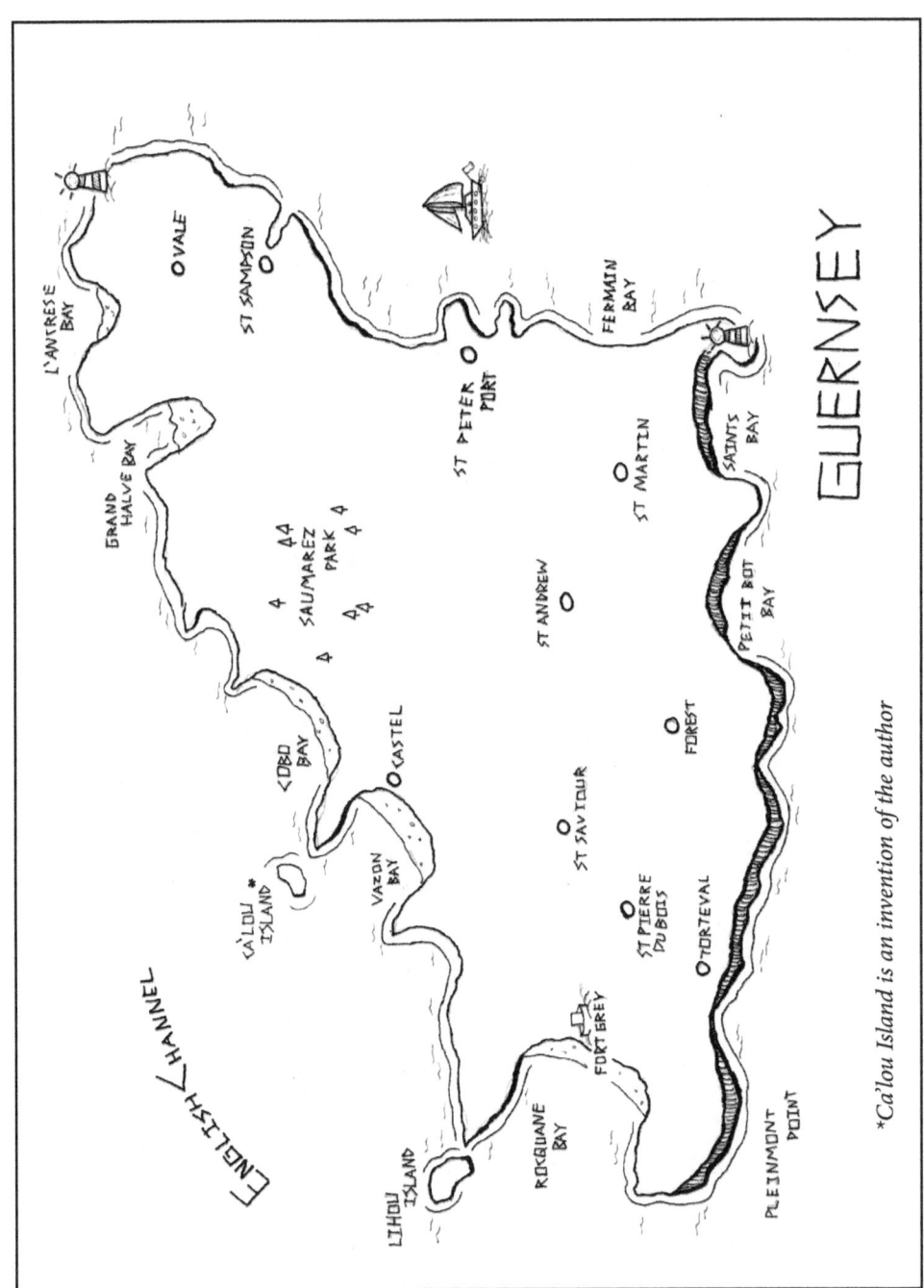

GUERNSEY

ENGLISH CHANNEL

L'ANCRESSE BAY

OVALE

ST SAMPSON

GRAND HAVRE BAY

SAUMAREZ PARK

COBO BAY

*CA'LOU ISLAND

KASTEL

VAZON BAY

LIHOU ISLAND

ROCQUAINE BAY

FORT GREY

ST PIERRE DUBOIS

ST SAVIOUR

ST ANDREW

FOREST

TORTEVAL

PLEINMONT POINT

ST PETER PORT

FERMAIN BAY

ST MARTIN

SAINTS BAY

PETIT BOT BAY

*Ca'lou Island is an invention of the author

Chapter One

"Wow!" exclaimed Antoinette as she put down the phone. "Oh, James! James! Where are you? Come up to the office!" There was no reply and she set off to find him. He didn't appear to be anywhere in the gallery, so she went outside to see if he was there, thinking he would be sitting looking over the harbour; something he often did when he needed to think. But he wasn't there either. "Typical when I really need to speak to him," she said. Excitement was bubbling away inside her. Where was he? She reached him by phone.

"Where are you, James?"

"I'm just having a coffee down at Amelia's, that little outside café on Fisherman's Wharf."

"Can you come back to the gallery? Now!"

"Of course. You sound excited, Annie – what is it?"

"I can't tell you on the phone, but I have some fantastic news."

He was back at the gallery in just a few minutes and Antoinette was waiting for him at the door. She grabbed his hand and quickly pulled him in and up to the office. The excitement was too much.

"James, it's fantastic, you will never guess who has just phoned."

"Your mother, your brother, the King?"

"Don't be flippant, this is serious."

"OK, OK! Come on then, tell me. I haven't seen you so excited, not for ages. What is it?"

"You've heard of Raphael Harcourt-Smythe, haven't you?"

"Heard of him! Antoinette, of course I've heard of him. He's one of the most famous and saleable contemporary artists in the world. Everybody's heard of him, I imagine, but what has he got to do with us?"

1

Antoinette grinned. "He wants to hold an exhibition here, at La Perle. What do you think of that?"

James became very quiet. He couldn't take in what she had just said. He didn't know what to say. "No, don't be silly," he finally responded. "You're joking with me."

"No," countered Antoinette. "Do I look as if I'm joking?"

"No, not really." He was still confused.

"So you don't believe me then," replied Antoinette huffily.

"It isn't that – I just can't believe it, that's all. I mean, he has the pick of all the major galleries, so why on earth would he want to come here? Why choose us? We might have a lovely little gallery here, but it isn't exactly the centre of the art world. London, Paris, New York… Guernsey! It doesn't quite ring true, does it?"

Antoinette was still offended.

"I'm sorry," he said. "I'm just being realistic; to me there must be a catch."

"OK," Antoinette conceded. "I thought the same at first, but I spoke to him for quite a while and it is genuine, honestly." She smiled. "I asked him all the same questions as you and he assured me he is totally serious."

"Why, though?" asked James. He still didn't understand the motivation of such a famous artist.

"I asked him that too. Apparently, some time ago – I don't know when – his father was rescued by the Guernsey Lifeboat crew, in the sea here just off St Peter Port. He promised he would do something for them by way of thanks. Some money, and also the profit from the sale of one of his paintings, is to go to the Guernsey Lifeboat Fund."

"I suppose that is some sort of motive," James agreed grudgingly.

"He also said it would be good publicity for him, to be seen as a wealthy artist but generous to good causes too."

James scoffed. "As if he needs the publicity!"

"Of course, he doesn't, but James – we do. What would the publicity and prestige do for us?"

"Oh, Antoinette, you are right. It still seems too good to be true, though."

"No James, it isn't, it's real. We are going to host an exhibition for this world-famous artist here, at La Perle, on the gorgeous little island of Guernsey."

Then James broke into a huge grin, convinced at last, but still not believing they could be so lucky. He gave Antoinette a big hug, then felt slightly overcome.

"I need to sit down, Annie. Is there some strong drink in that little cabinet of yours?"

"I'll join you," and she poured two large single malts. "Here's to us, our little gallery and future successes." James drank his almost in one go.

"Oh, Annie, we never could have imagined this, ever."

To say that they had a scoop was an understatement. La Perle was indeed a small and lovely art gallery. It was situated on the old Fisherman's Wharf, now gentrified but retaining its character and atmosphere. It had kept the old cobbles and had become pedestrianised, which led to the development of an artisans' enclave. There were bars too, delicatessens, up-market shops, studios, cafés and restaurants, many with outdoor seating and some with first-floor balconies looking out over the wharf and harbour. The ambiance was one of exclusivity, the place where people liked to be seen. It was only just outside the capital, St Peter Port, but had its own identity and character, enhanced by old lobster pots, old tarry rope and the scent of a salty sea. It was an ideal spot for a gallery, though it was still quite early days for Antoinette and James, who were having to work hard to build their reputation. Now, it was possible that their reputation was made.

* * *

The next day, both of them were still stunned and wondering about the reality of it all.

"We're running before we can walk," Antoinette said. "He's completely out of our league. And then there is security, insurance, publicity, not to mention finding the money to set it all up. Of course, there would be fees and commissions, but we'll have to find the curating money first." She was anxious and fidgeting. The excitement of the previous day had been superseded by the reality of it all.

"Now who's looking for problems?" James walked over to her desk and spoke reassuringly. "Look, we may be a small provincial gallery, but we aren't novices. We have expertise and talent, and we do know how to host an exhibition. This one will just be a bit more scary, that's all," he said with a laugh. "The method is exactly the same." Whether he felt as confident as he appeared was unlikely, but it did help Antoinette.

"Yes, you're right. You always manage to reassure and convince me. But James, you really are going to have to spend more time here to help me and keep my feet on the ground."

"You know I will. I'll work around my own job, don't worry. It's still early days too. He might change his mind. We just don't know. Let's wait until we've met him and take it from there."

"Oh, you are always so sensible, but it is exciting isn't it?"

"Annie, it's absolutely wonderful. It is the best thing that could ever have happened to La Perle and I'm just hoping it won't unravel."

"It won't, James, it won't. I have a good feeling about it." Antoinette put her mug of coffee down on the desk and walked over to James who was looking out of the window. She put her arms around him. "Thank you so much – I don't know what I would do without you. The gallery would never have happened without your investment and commitment. You have always encouraged me". There were tears in her eyes and he held her close.

"You don't need to thank me, you know that, and it was a great investment; this gallery is going to be a great success," he said, at which Antoinette smiled. "Anyway," continued James, "seeing you so happy is repayment in itself. However, I now need to go to work, but we could meet for a late lunch?"

"That would be great. I'm so churned up; I can't concentrate on anything here. Eleanor is in today so I can leave her in charge and enjoy a nice long lunch."

* * *

James Kerrissey was not a Guernseyman; he was a London exile. At Exeter University he had met Gabriel and they had become good friends. After graduation, Gabriel couldn't wait to return to his home on Guernsey where he had been born and brought up. He invited James to visit, which he did on several occasions, liking the island that was so very different to his urban lifestyle. Gabriel later suggested he might like to come and live in the Channel Islands.

"Oh, Gabriel, I'm not sure. It's lovely but I'm an urbanite, well and truly. I don't know if I could live on the island permanently."

"But there are some great opportunities," persisted Gabriel. "You're already in financial service – it would suit you. Why not give it a try, even just for a year?"

"Oh, I don't know, Gabriel. I'll think about it."

"I can look out for a job for you," Gabriel encouraged.

Think James did, and tried it he did, and to his surprise he really liked it and stayed. He now couldn't foresee that he would ever leave. Yes, it had proved a very different life, but he had come to love it. Yes, the island was small, only nine miles by three, but, unlike many Scottish islands for example, it was not windswept, treeless and under-populated. It was just the opposite. With a population of around 60,000, parts of the island – especially around St Peter Port – were built up, yet there were many other areas that were still quiet and even remote; beautiful, with many different beaches and cliff walks. Generally, the island was green and leafy, quite mellow, and often bathed in sunshine which, given its close proximity to France, made it feel continental, and the French influence was evident across the island. At work, he now sat at his desk and reflected on how his life had turned out. He could never have imagined a life in Guernsey and now here he was, a partner in an art gallery with Gabriel's sister Antoinette and with a never-imagined major exhibition to plan. It was more than he or Antoinette could ever have dared to hope.

* * *

Over the next few weeks, they both held their breath and tried not to think about all the 'what ifs', and after four weeks Raphael again phoned La Perle. He assured Antoinette that he had no intention of changing his mind. "Oh, my dear!" he exclaimed when Antoinette asked if the exhibition was still going ahead. "Of course it is. Once I've made a decision, I rarely change it. Indeed, I am rather excited at the prospect of coming over to your little island, which is why I am ringing today. My agent, Constantin, would like to meet you next week and talk over some of my ideas. How does that sound, darling? Can we arrange something? He'll make all his own flight and hotel arrangements."

"That'll be great. I'm really looking forward to our planning meetings, and even more to meeting Constantin and yourself, Mr Harcourt-Smythe. My partner, James, and I are confident you will find everything here will be absolutely fine."

"That's super then, darling Antoinette, and do call me Raphael."

Antoinette put the phone down, flustered and hot, but completely excited. Unlike James, Antoinette had lived all her life on Guernsey apart from her university years. Her close and extended family still lived on the island too. Her years studying at St Martin's and The Slade had developed her art skills. It showed her, too, how very different life in the capital city was from her beloved Guernsey. Her qualification had been worth the years in London, but she'd been desperate to return home.

Like her brother Gabriel, Antoinette Duchenne couldn't imagine ever living anywhere other than her precious Guernsey. Her art skills were good, but she was realistic, knowing that it would be hard to pursue a professional artist's life, and she had decided to further her education by pursuing a course in art curating. She knew another string to her bow would help her, and so it had proved.

James and Antoinette offered to meet Constantin at the airport, but he insisted on first settling in at the hotel and then meeting them at the gallery. The plan was to relax over coffee, show him around the gallery and Fisherman's Wharf, then mellow him with a long lunch. Hopefully, he would leave convinced that La Perle was the perfect venue.

"Oh, James, I am so nervous. I just can't keep still. I do wish he would come." She found herself walking up and down the gallery, her nerves frayed.

"I'm nervous too," concurred James, "but it's exciting, isn't it?"

Antoinette was too keyed up to be excited. "Are we sure of everything we need to tell him?"

"We've been over it endlessly, Annie, so please calm down. My biggest worry is what he will ask us; hopefully he won't want to catch us out with things we haven't thought of. But at the end of the day, we need to remember that they contacted us, not the other way round. I can't believe they would want to trick us or make it awkward. What would be the point? Raphael wanted it to work – he's already made up his mind."

"You're right, so let's be confident. This may not be London, but we do know what we are doing."

"Exactly," James said firmly, "so now will you please stop pacing, you're making me dizzy."

"Sorry," she said and they both smiled.

* * *

"Is anyone around?" came a voice from the entrance. "This is Constantin – can I come through?"

"Here we are, Constantin," said Antoinette and they both went to join him, Antoinette with fingers firmly crossed.

"So, you found us OK," said James as he held out his hand to shake Constantin's. "Good to meet you." Constantin gripped his hand firmly. "We are really looking forward to working with you and Raphael," continued James.

"So, you must be Antoinette," said Constantin, smiling broadly and vigorously shaking her hand.

"Absolutely wonderful to meet you," Antoinette replied. "Come up to the office; we have coffee ready if you would like some, or tea if you prefer."

"Coffee will be great, thank you," he said as he followed them up the stairs.

"He seems nice," Antoinette said to herself, "not snobbish as I thought he might be."

She looked at James wondering if he was thinking the same, but his expression seemed unusually inscrutable. The office was small but stylish with pale oak floors and a large window that opened on to a small balcony, from where the sun was streaming in. Constantin walked out on to the balcony and stood enjoying the lovely views out to the harbour.

"This is lovely – what a beautiful view. If the rest of the gallery is like this then we have nothing to worry about."

Antoinette and James, sitting primly, beamed at each other. This had started well, very well indeed.

Constantin left the balcony, came back into the office and sat down. "Did you convert the gallery yourselves?"

"Not with our very own hands," Antoinette explained "but we had it converted for us from an old warehouse. It was ideal because it enabled us to keep the double height which gives the gallery a real sense of space and atmosphere. Come on, we'll show you around, and then we can sit outside on our little balcony while we talk."

Constantin followed them into the gallery. James noticed he seemed to be captivated by Antoinette, which he knew was perfectly understandable, for she was not only beautiful, but had poise, charisma and enthusiasm by the bucketload. She endeared herself to people, a great asset when running a business. Antoinette, however, was generally oblivious to her effect: she was just being herself. In the meantime, he studied Constantin. He was tall, with dark, slightly curly hair and an olive complexion. He was the type who, however often they shaved, always had a hint of a five o'clock shadow. His eyes were dark and deep-set, but his mouth and smile had a softness, almost a gentleness about them. James had no doubt that women could easily be attracted to him.

They strolled around the gallery, Constantin quiet as he took everything in. The gallery, compared to many others, was small, with one display room, but it was double height and full of light. Above was a mezzanine along one side where a small café looked out, partly over the exhibition area and also out over the harbour, complete with a small balcony containing a couple of tables and chairs. It was a popular spot for customers.

"Will it be suitable, do you think?" queried Antoinette nervously. "Will there be enough space? We don't really know what Raphael wants, or even how many paintings he wants to display." She found herself rambling a little, desperate to please.

James, seeing her nervousness, stepped in. "We are confident we can make it work, Constantin."

"Don't be so worried, you two. I think your gallery is exceptional. It's beautiful, it's contemporary, and it's exactly the type of space Raphael is looking for. You have done a wonderful job here."

James saw Antoinette relax and he smiled. "Thank you," he said.

"You see," continued Constantin, "we don't need acres of empty wall. Raphael's method is in effect and impact, not in volume. We will probably expect to have a few large canvasses on the walls and a few exhibits hanging from the mezzanine so they can be viewed from the café. And I need to tell you that Raphael's intention is to showcase his new canvas, 'Madrigal', which will not be on a wall but suspended from the ceiling into the lower room. It will make a fantastic dramatic image. Yes, it will be perfect; I can see it all very clearly."

"That's wonderful!" exclaimed James. "It sounds amazing! How lucky are we that one of Britain's foremost artists wants to exhibit his newest work here? I'm still unsure how we've come to deserve it."

"But you have, James," reassured Constantin, "and believe me Raphael didn't just put any old names in the hat. Once I've spoken to him he will be one hundred percent certain this is the right place for his special exhibition in recognition of the lifeboat service. You do know that one of his paintings, when sold, will be a gift for the lifeboat fund? Not 'Madrigal' but one of the others."

"It's such a generous thing to do," Antoinette said, "and it will probably be a huge amount too."

"Certainly it will, possibly a million pounds."

James and Antoinette lapsed into a stunned silence, barely able to believe what they were hearing. It suddenly occurred to Antoinette that they, too, were likely to make a lot of money themselves. "Oh, heavens! That means we will make money in commission on all his sales. Is that right, Constantin?"

"Of course you will, if we can agree on a commission of twenty percent."

Antoinette suddenly felt very faint. They had been standing in the gallery and she had to find a chair. James, too, felt none too steady.

"How strange," James whispered. "We knew this exhibition would make our reputation; how ridiculous it never occurred to us it could also make us a lot of money!"

"Then believe it now," confirmed Constantin. "All his paintings command exceptional prices but he hopes 'Madrigal will sell for around five to ten million pounds."

After the initial shock they both became giddy with excitement, disbelief, and elation, all rolled in together.

They all went for a lovely, relaxed lunch, taking Constantin to one of Guernsey's best restaurants, situated high on a cliff and offering spectacular views along the coast and over towards the small island of Herm. Florian's was always popular and it was great to share the good food and atmosphere with Constantin. They were already confident, but top-quality food and champagne could only enhance their good fortune. The next hurdle, of course, would be to meet Raphael, but the wine, atmosphere and Constantin's optimism allayed their fears.

Constantin asked no more questions about the exhibition but wanted to know more about Antoinette and James: he seemed genuinely interested.

"Have you always lived here, Antoinette?"

"Yes, it's my family home and I love it here. I couldn't wait to get back here after university. I wasn't sure what I was going to do and then when James helped finance La Perle it worked out perfectly. I have a little flat above the gallery and the wonderful views compensate for its size."

"It sounds like you have found what you want. Not many people do – you're lucky."

"I know. Thank you, Constantin."

"And you, James, you aren't a Guernseyman?"

"No, I'm a fairly new resident. I work in financial services, as do many others here," he said with a laugh. "And I can help out at the gallery too, of course."

"And I see you work well as business partners?"

"We're really good friends too, and that helps," confirmed Antoinette.

"I'm so looking forward to working with you." His words were genuine and reassuring. "Now, as regards Raphael," he continued, "he hopes to come over in a couple of weeks to make some final decisions and confirm the date for the exhibition, which we know will be around the end of August. I'll leave you to your celebrations now – it's been a long day. Thank you for the delicious meal. Don't worry, Raphael will call; he's a busy person as you can imagine, but I can assure you there is no doubt about the exhibition, believe me." He gave a little wave as he left the room, but more than that, his smile was warm, leaving James and Antoinette beaming with pleasure.

* * *

Later, back in his office, James' phone rang.

"Was it a dream, James?" asked Antoinette, "or did we just meet in our gallery and discover we may soon be millionaires?"

Laughing, James replied "No, Annie sweetheart, I think it was real, or else we had the same dream. Hard to believe though, isn't it?"

"That's a bit of an understatement! Have you worked out twenty percent of ten million? Good grief! I knew his paintings sold well, but can he really be expecting one picture to sell for such a vast sum?"

"Look on the internet, sweetie – his prices seem to be going up and up. I'm not sure I should be saying this as we'll benefit, but I'm unsure why they are so valuable. Even if he is a brilliant artist, would you pay ten million?"

"I couldn't afford to, James, but I'm certainly glad someone can."

Chapter Two

James had first met Antoinette when she visited Gabriel at Exeter University. He was an undergraduate there, while Antoinette was still taking her GCSEs. Gabriel was very protective of his sister. He clearly loved and really missed her when he left home to go to Exeter. In talents and temperament, they were entirely different. Gabriel was quiet and studious, while Antoinette was lively, expressive and artistic. James could see how their careers would go in entirely different directions; but wherever it took them, they would never lose contact or their love for each other. Quite when James fell in love with Antoinette he couldn't now say, but as time went by and she turned into a clever and beautiful woman, he knew he was deeply in love with her. He admitted, too, that the reason he'd agreed to live on Guernsey was because of Antoinette. When he had settled on the island and she came back from her studies, his feelings hadn't changed. As for Antoinette's feelings, he just didn't know. They got on well and socialised with the same people, but he realised she only loved him as a friend, almost an extension of her brother. Plus, she was young, enthusiastic about her new life and enjoying her freedom and independence. He could wait, having her as a true and loving friend was enough at the time. Any relationships he'd had, though, proved unsatisfactory and his feelings always returned to Antoinette.

He was in his office, dreaming, and he roused himself and went for some fresh air to bring his mind back to the here and now.

Antoinette was still finding it hard to come down to earth, and she was deliberately trying to calm herself down. She had an exhibition already in place, and so had a responsibility to the artist to try her best to bring in the customers and sell as many of the paintings as she could. Walking slowly around the gallery, she noticed a new red dot. 'Another one sold, that's good,' she told herself. By any artistic standards, the paintings were somewhat unspectacular, although the artist did have technical ability. It was just that they were like so many others, pretty watercolours, mostly Guernsey landscapes. She would have liked something with a bit more flair and individuality, not to say a different subject matter. 'But then again,' she admitted to herself, 'the tourists like them and are keen to take them home as souvenirs. It would be foolish of me to ignore such exhibitions; they are the gallery's bread and butter.'

"Eleanor," she called, as she went into the office. "I see there's another picture sold."

"Yes, it was yesterday when you were at lunch," her assistant explained. "It's good, isn't it?"

"Yes, great! We've sold quite a few now, which is good so early in the season. But Eleanor, the future looks so promising" she said and told her about Constantin and his reassurance that the exhibition would definitely go ahead.

"Oh, Annie, that is so wonderful!" Eleanor smiled radiantly.

"I know. We could hardly believe it – I haven't come down to earth yet."

"I'm not surprised. You will let me meet Raphael, won't you?"

"Of course, you idiot. You'll be part of the whole event. And, if you're lucky, you could be in for a nice fat bonus."

"Yeah!" exclaimed Eleanor. "That will certainly help me pay off some of my university debts."

"Yes it will, but suspend your excitement just for now."

"I will, I won't let it go to my head."

Antoinette knew it already had, as she almost skipped from the office, a real spring in her step. She smiled; she was lucky to have such a lovely, trustworthy assistant.

Antoinette sat down to work. She had another exhibition to stage before Raphael's and she would really need to concentrate to put it all in place. This exhibition was to comprise a group of local artists, with a planned start date for June, and lasting one month. That still allowed plenty of time to plan 'Madrigal', which was now the title of Raphael's exhibition. It seemed enigmatic, and he had given no clues as to its meaning, which would no doubt unfold as time went on. Would there be some medieval music and dancing, she wondered? No, don't be silly, but still no other interpretation came to mind. She picked up the phone to call James but there was no reply, so she followed with a text. 'How are you feeling?' They hadn't spoken since their meeting with Constantin, and she suddenly really wanted to speak to him. The reality seemed quite overwhelming. On top of this, Antoinette knew that, without James, none of this could have happened. Even now, two years on, she still found it hard to understand why he had been so keen to be not just her business partner, but also to risk such a large amount of money on the gallery. After all, there was no guarantee that La Perle would be successful; absolutely none at all. He had told her he had inherited the money and that the gallery was an investment. Even so, few people would have had the faith or courage to take on such a venture. And yet, so far it had worked. They were already friends, and now, as business partners, they seemed to have found a perfect working relationship. He worked in his finance enclave while she ran the gallery and James helped when necessary, made possible because of his current self-employed status. He also continued paying bills and wages, as La Perle was not yet fully paying its way into real profit. She was amazed at his generosity and would be eternally grateful to him. She hoped that she could find a way to repay his kindness.

* * *

Spring often came early to Guernsey and, as the lanes greened up, the gorse on the cliffs blossomed and wild flowers were in profusion in the hedgerows. On a warm day, the heady coconut scent of the gorse gave the island a distinctly Mediterranean feel. With spring too, the island became noticeably busier, with more fleeting cruise-ship visitors, as well as those tourists staying for a while longer. James realised early on that it was worth nurturing the cruise liners, whereby he spent time persuading their tourist guides to include a visit to La Perle in their packed itineraries. It had worked too, better than they could have hoped. But Antoinette knew that much of James' persuasion took the form of banknotes crossing palms.

* * *

It was on a dull spring day when Constantin phoned to say that, as promised, Raphael would like to visit the following weekend.

"Will that be convenient?"

"Of course it will!" Antoinette gushed. This announcement sent James and Antoinette into another flurry of excitement. Then, after calming down, they organised a planning meeting the next day. They sat upstairs in their little café, looking out to sea and watching the yachts taking advantage of the weather. It was dull, fairly calm, with just a gentle breeze, almost perfect sailing weather.

"It's actually quite hard to know how to plan, isn't it?" said Antoinette.

"Yes, it is rather," agreed James. "We have absolutely no idea what to expect. We don't know what he's like, what kind of gallery he wants, or what he expects of us." They talked round and round the subject, but in the end, both knew there was little they could do.

"At the end of the day he'll either like us and our gallery, or not, and we can't change either."

Antoinette agreed. "But there is one thing I can plan," she said, giving James a huge grin.

"What? What's so funny?"

"Nothing, but I'm going to treat myself to a pampering day, an expensive facial and a gorgeous new dress. How about you?"

"Well, I don't need a new dress, but I might take you up on the facial!" he said and he laughed too. Antoinette dug him in the ribs.

"Idiot, you know what I mean."

"No, I honestly don't. What is it I'm supposed to do?"

"Well, I don't know," Antoinette admitted. "I suppose whatever a man does to prepare for a special event."

"Mmm, I need to think about that. When are you thinking of booking this pampering day?"

"James, I thought of it days ago, it's already booked. Victoria and Madeleine are coming too. We're going to have a fabulous girls' day out."

"In that case I might arrange something with Gabriel. It seems ages since we had a drink together."

* * *

The Guernsey Jewel was one of the most expensive hotels on the island, situated in St Peter Port, a little gem of a town, small but perfectly formed. Approached from the sea on a sunny day, it had the look and ambience of a Mediterranean port, with rows of colourful buildings lining the waterfront and rising up in terraces to the old upper town. The magnificent Castle Cornet, and its famous booming midday gun, stood sentinel and proud at the end of the marina. The Guernsey Jewel lacked coastal views, but made up for it with its fabulous spa and its reputation as one of the most select restaurants on the island. Its opulence, fine food and spa treatments confirmed its popularity throughout the year.

Antoinette, Victoria and Maddy had booked in for a morning of swimming, sauna and all the spa's other attractions, followed by lunch and then spa treatments in the afternoon. All three had swallowed hard when they realised the cost and were determined to benefit from the luxury they had paid for. At lunchtime they were relaxing in the spa restaurant in their fluffy bathrobes, faces flushed with pleasure.

"This is absolutely fantastic!" gushed Victoria. "Why don't we do this more often?"

"I wish," Madeline answered. "It's so relaxing. I feel miles away from the outside world."

"Well, I'm starving," Antoinette commented. "All that swimming has really worked up an appetite."

"Me too," echoed Victoria.

"Oh, here's lunch now." Antoinette looked longingly at the plates the waitress brought. She was pleased to note that, although the food was healthy looking, there was plenty of it, and there were yummy puddings too.

"Oh, it looks fabulous!" Antoinette laughed and eagerly tucked into her salmon fillet. All was calm and relaxed. They had plenty of time to enjoy their food before it was time for their facials and other therapies. Maddy was intrigued by the other guests.

"It's busy, isn't it, especially for mid-week?" she said, acknowledging the groups of women laughing and enjoying their glasses of wine, with seemingly no concern for time. "Does nobody work?" she continued, a little confused.

"Maddy," laughed Victoria, "we're here and we work. It's called a day off."

"Course, that's true," conceded Maddy.

"And…" Antoinette added, in a somewhat quieter voice, "…probably most of these women don't need to work; ladies who lunch and all that."

"Lucky them. I think I could manage this every week, and lunch with my friends," Victoria replied with a faraway look in her eyes.

"Could you, though? Really?" Antoinette questioned. "I'm not sure it would suit me. I enjoy my life and independence and it's satisfying."

"You could be right," agreed Victoria, "but some of their money might be nice."

"Anyway, come on. I want to know about this Raphael. After all, that is why we're here, isn't it?" questioned Maddy with a twinkle in her eyes.

Antoinette blushed. "That's not true. I just thought that a nice relaxing day would calm me down before we meet."

"Oh, right," scoffed Victoria, "so it has nothing at all to do with wanting to look exquisite for a meeting with one of the richest and most famous artists in the world? I have to admit that with a name like Raphael Harcourt-Smythe, I rather think I might make a special effort too."

"It's nothing like that," stressed Antoinette, but then they all burst into laughter. "Oh, you're right, I just can't wait to meet him."

"I imagine he must be rather posh as well as very rich. He probably has a family pedigree going back for generations. Does he?"

"Actually, I honestly don't know anything about his background, it's all been very much business up to now. No doubt, though, he has the temperament that goes with being so famous. I don't want to upset him – we really want this exhibition. It could be the making of La Perle."

"You bet," agreed Victoria.

* * *

James had made rather less of an effort, but he was content to meet for a drink. He desperately wanted the exhibition but found himself somewhat unconcerned about the artist himself. He sensed that he would either like their little gallery or not, and there really was very little they could do about it. But for Annie's sake he could not imagine the scenario where Raphael said no. He knew how desperate she was about La Perle hosting such a prestigious exhibition. Gabriel was keen to hear about it all and didn't hesitate in accepting James' offer of an evening in the pub. They hadn't met up for ages and he knew they would enjoy it. They chose an old, noisy pub, popular for its hand-pumped beer and its 'beers of the month'. It was a struggle to have a decent conversation, but the beer was worth it. As they were leaving, Gabriel said he hoped to be able to meet Raphael.

"No problem. I'm sure we can sort something out; we can perhaps all get together for a meal."

James had no idea how his optimism would be completely unfounded.

* * *

Constantin phoned to say that he and Raphael were just finishing breakfast, and would then be on their way. "Is everything okay there?" he asked.

"Fine, unless you think we may have forgotten something?" Antoinette asked anxiously.

"No, no, after all we've discussed, I can't think of anything. But I wanted to reassure you and tell you not to worry," said Constantin soothingly. "The only thing is, have you got the champagne chilling? He does love his lunchtime glass."

Laughing, Antoinette confirmed "Oh yes, it's well chilled."

"See you shortly then."

* * *

"Well James, if cold champagne is his main concern, we don't seem to have much to be anxious about."

"Let's hope so – we've done everything he asked for. The only things left are to curtsey and salute."

"Honestly, James, you do say some silly things."

In fact, it was very late morning when Raphael and Constantin arrived, by which time, after pacing up and down, Antoinette was in a very nervous state.

"Are you sure I look OK? You seem so calm and suave in your new bespoke suit. Very handsome."

"Antoinette, you always look lovely, and you couldn't have chosen a better outfit. Glamorous, but business-like too, and I really like your hair swept up." In fact, he had already noticed that her lemon silk day dress enhanced her rich auburn hair and, with sparkling diamond earrings setting off her shining eyes, he thought she had never looked so beautiful. Then there came noises from the entrance, and they were in no doubt that Raphael had arrived.

"Constantin, I thought we would never get here." Raphael's voice was loud and affected. "I do so hope it is worth it after so much preparation." His voice now was high with anxiety.

"It's going to be fine," soothed Constantin.

"I do hope so."

"Stop and take a deep breath, Raphael – the owners have done everything to please you, so stop worrying."

"I never worry – that's your job, Constantin." Constantin sighed and rolled his eyes. "Now, what is the man's name again?"

Constantin whispered to him and their voices faded. Antoinette and James stood and looked at each other, consternation clear on their faces.

"Does he think we can't hear them?" James said, confused.

"Ssh, they're coming now. Quick, walk over to the stairs so they think we have only just come down."

James immediately felt sorry for Constantin. How hard must it be to work for such a highly strung person. But now there was no more waiting and Antoinette and James fixed a big smile on their faces.

"Here we go," he said, and walked forward as Raphael and Constantin finally entered the gallery.

"Antoinette, my darling," Raphael gushed as he swept across the floor. "I can't tell you how much I have been looking forward to meeting you." He greeted her with air kisses. "Oh, yes, you are everything I expected, darling – so poised, so beautiful, so professional." He held her at arm's length. "Oh yes, just as I thought, we will have such a wonderful partnership." Then he looked around. "Oh yes, this gallery is divine! It's so absolutely perfect."

Antoinette blushed, looked embarrassed at James, unsure how to respond to this famous man and his exaggerated manners. In the meantime, James stood idly by, wondering when Raphael would deign to speak to him. Constantin, too, looked rather embarrassed.

James compared the two men. Constantin tall, olive skinned, dark hair and deep brown eyes, crinkled at the edges. Raphael was the opposite: slightly less then medium height, blondish ruffled hair, unremarkable blue-grey coloured eyes and wearing flamboyant clothes in mis-matched bright colours. He had an altogether Bohemian appearance, yet he gave off such an air of confidence and self-importance that he was immediately lifted above the ordinary, and he knew it too. James had to look away; he knew immediately that he could never like this man.

"Well, thank you, Raphael. I am so excited, I can't tell you how much we are looking forward to working with you," James heard Antoinette reply.

"I'm sure you are," Raphael replied. "My exhibitions are always a great success; anyone would consider it an honour to be able to hold one."

"Oh yes," Antoinette agreed, abashed at his confidence and yet consumed by his presence. She tried to move the conversation on. "Constantin tells me you like your champagne, so why don't we all go up to the office? We can sip some bubbly, sitting on our balcony looking over the wharf. And you need to meet James too – we are equal partners. I couldn't run this place without him. Come on James, Constantin, let's go and open the bottle and celebrate."

"Oh yes, I must meet him."

Reluctantly, James followed but was angry that, up to now, he had been completely ignored.

Antoinette led Raphael on to the balcony. Constantin held back and James took responsibility for the champagne. He was far from impressed, yet he knew the future of their gallery depended on this man and the exhibition's success. He relaxed, fixed a smile on his face, and moved to offer Raphael a glass of champagne.

"Champagne, Raphael? It's good to meet you," he said, offering the glass to Raphael and his hand to shake. Raphael grabbed the glass, responded with a curt thanks and went straight back to Antoinette to enjoy the view. It was a beautiful day, the wharfside wasn't so much noisy as buzzing with atmosphere, with locals as well as tourists, strolling or sitting at the outside cafes enjoying the day.

"What a gorgeous view, my dearest Antoinette," Raphael enthused.

"How do you tear yourself away to do any work?" he continued, his voice mellifluous and captivating. "It is magnificent here." He continued to admire the view. After a couple of minutes, he pointed out to sea. "Is that the lifeboat I see out in the bay, my darling?"

"Yes, it will be on a practise run out of St Peter Port."

"I must make a date to introduce myself. They will be so excited to meet me, their new benefactor. But that will have to wait for another day. Come, Antoinette, show me the rest of your exquisite little gallery – we must make our plans. Constantin, come on, let's get those measurements done. Is there any more champagne, James? Another glass please!" he commanded as he moved out and down the stairs to the main gallery space. James gritted his teeth, topped up the champagne and handed Raphael his refilled glass. James muttered under his breath. 'Yes, sir, anything you like, sir. Kiss your backside, sir?'

As Raphael moved around the gallery, Antoinette beckoned James to follow. She looked nervous and, not wanting to cause any upset, he slowly followed, although to say he was less than happy was an understatement. He knew he would have to find a way to work alongside this rude, arrogant man, but it wasn't going to be easy.

Antoinette escorted Raphael, whilst Constantin and James lagged behind. James felt left out, quite abandoned, yet it wasn't Antoinette's fault. She realised that James wasn't part of the tour.

"Raphael, hold on a moment, let James catch up with us. There is so much he can tell you that I don't know." She moved to James' side, ushered him along, smiling and taking his hand.

"Hurry up and join us then, James!" said Raphael, "though I'm sure our lovely Antoinette can tell me all I need to know." He reached out, put his arm around her shoulder and pulled her away from James. He sauntered around as if there were just the two of them in the room. Constantin, meanwhile, had wandered off to finalise measurements. He didn't know what to say. His employer could be so embarrassing and irritating, but he knew to hold his tongue. James was flushed with anger, and more than a little jealous. He retreated to the other side of the room.

Still nervous, Antoinette stole a glance at James. She was perplexed, confused, but felt compelled by Raphael's audacity and overpowering control. Timidly she asked if he was happy with the gallery and if he was confident that the exhibition would go ahead.

"Of course, my sweet. Constantin has already confirmed to me that all was satisfactory. I can't imagine a more suitable, gorgeous little gallery. Everyone will want to come, believe me – everyone."

She visibly relaxed and gave a sigh of relief. She looked to James to reassure him but he wasn't looking at her; his thoughts seemed far away.

"Now, Constantin and I need to leave you. We have much to discuss."

As they approached the front door, he put his arm around Antoinette, kissed her hand, and then they were both gone. She stood by the door and waved as she watched them wander down the wharf. Back inside, flushed and overcome, she admitted to herself it had been something of an ordeal, yet at the same time he had impressed her. His confidence made her feel so sure about the exhibition, giving her hope that this really would be the making of La Perle. Before she came back into the gallery, James disappeared into the gents and then, as he heard her walk back up to the office, he quietly left and went back to his office in town. His phone rang almost immediately and he knew it would be Antoinette.

"James, where are you? What's wrong? Why did you sneak off like that? You didn't even say goodbye to Raphael. What were you thinking?"

James knew she was upset but so was he, and his reply was unusually curt. "Why? Do you really need me to explain?"

"Yes. I don't understand. What is wrong with you?"

"Wrong with me?" he countered. "There is nothing wrong with me. It's that pompous, rude, darling Raphael that has the problem, not me! Darling this, sweetheart that; he was far too forward with you. He'd only just met you, for goodness' sake. So unprofessional too and slimy."

"He's an artist, James, it's the temperament. Don't be silly, it's just how he is."

"Well, I don't like how he is. He's ignorant! He completely ignored me all afternoon. There is no need for such behaviour, artist or not."

"But we've got to work with him, James, haven't we?"

"Yes, okay, but I don't have to like him."

"You haven't given him a chance."

"I don't want to give him a chance, but I can see he has already won his way into your affections."

"Don't be so stubborn, James. Before they left, Constantin said he and Raphael would like us to join them for dinner to discuss the contract. Won't you come?"

"No, he won't be bothered about me as long as you're there. You agree the deal with him; I trust you and I'll support whatever you decide."

"Please, James."

"No, Annie," he said and put the phone down. It was the first time he could ever remember them arguing, either about business or personal issues. He was upset, ruffled, angry. But he was also uneasy and concerned, not quite knowing why. He knew this was their opportunity of a lifetime. Perhaps it was just his temperament. He trusted Antoinette and knew she would broker the best deal. He convinced himself about this, but deep down he knew he was using it as an excuse not to be involved. Over the next few days, he only attended certain necessary business meetings about the exhibition, meetings he couldn't really avoid. But the atmosphere was strained, and Antoinette seemed distant, more than he had ever known her to be. He was unhappy and wished that Antoinette had never picked up the phone to Raphael. At the same time, he knew he was being sulky and irrational, and felt worse that Antoinette seemed to be getting along fine without him.

Antoinette seemed to have fallen under Raphael's spell. In her own defence, she would say that she was simply inspired by his legendary talent, his artistry, his presence. Privately, she admitted that she was overwhelmed by his power, his attention, his faith in himself, and his ability to inspire her with confidence, and promote the certainty that he could secure both her future and her fortune. She never questioned any of Raphael's motives, but she did wonder why, when he had the pick of rich and beautiful women, he was lavishing so much attention on her. She knew that, with his Bohemian clothes and looks, he wasn't the typical handsome man, but his attraction was his magnetism; his way of gliding across the room always attracting attention. Most of all, he could look across a room and smile at Antoinette so that it seemed no-one else was there. She knew she was on dangerous ground.

By the time Raphael was due back in Guernsey for his second visit, Antoinette and James had still not reconciled their differences, so Antoinette had been making the arrangements, and their plans were moving forward. She and Raphael had developed an easy working relationship, and it no longer seemed an ordeal dealing with his demands. Before he once more returned to London, Antoinette had booked a meal for them both. It was a beautiful evening, soft and balmy, and they retired after their meal to the outside terrace.

"You choose so well, my darling," said Raphael as he breathed in the sea air and listened to the waves gently lapping against the sand. "Where are we tonight? I haven't yet found my bearings on your island."

"We're on the north of the island, opposite Ca'lou beach, which is why this is the Ca-lou hotel. It isn't the smartest of restaurant, but it is in a fabulous spot."

"And what is the light I can see out across the water?" Raphael queried.

"That's Ca-lou island. There is a large sandy beach, popular with surfers, and the island can be reached at low tide across the causeway."

"Is it worth walking over to?"

"Well, it's very small, but it does have an interesting history. No-one lives there now but on one side there are the ruins of a monastery, never an important one, and I don't think there were ever more than a dozen monks there. It looks lovely when it's floodlit, doesn't it?"

"It does, but it's quite haunting too."

"I suppose it is. But the other side of the island is not quite so nice. There is a huge German bunker there, left from the war. They were so solidly built that it remains completely untouched; stark and monstrous. People don't like to go there. They say it has a horrible atmosphere, and it has a reputation of being haunted."

Raphael, a little confused, asked "But I thought a bunker was underground? This one isn't?"

"You're right, part of it is underground, but the part you can see above ground was a watchtower and what look like large open windows are gun emplacements; huge ledges jutting out over the sea. It gave the Germans a perfect view, and also great manoeuvrability for their guns."

"Were the guns ever fired?"

"No, well I don't think so anyway – thank goodness."

"Have you ever been there?"

"To the island, yes, lots of times, but I don't ever want to go into the bunker. On a sunny day, though, it's a perfect little island for a picnic."

"Will you take me there one day, Antoinette?"

"Of course."

"Come on, let's go for a stroll. It's such a gorgeous night."

The sky was clear and studded with stars, a bright half-moon bathing the sand in an ethereal glow. They walked along the sand towards the island, but the causeway was covered by the sea.

"We can't go any further tonight, but I'll check the tides for your next visit and we will be able to walk out there."

"That will be lovely. I am so looking forward to it."

Antoinette could not quite believe her romantic moonlight stroll with this famous, captivating man.

"Thank you, my sweet, for such a wonderful evening." Raphael stood and looked back at the little island, suddenly lost in his thoughts. "Yes, such a perfect place," he said. Breaking out of his reverie, he took Antoinette's arm and led her back to the restaurant.

* * *

James knew he was being stupid. He knew, too, that he hadn't put in as much time as he should have at the gallery. Yet he couldn't help how he felt. He didn't want to hurt Antoinette or to let her down; he would have to do something to make things right. He had tried with Raphael, he really had. Constantin, unlike Raphael, was aware of the tension and atmosphere, but didn't know what to do about it.

"James," Constantin said when they had all met at the gallery, "we're going back to London tomorrow. Is there anything you want to add before we go?"

Before James could reply, Raphael interrupted. "No, Constantin, there isn't anything else, and, anyway, I can always contact Antoinette from London, can't I, sweetheart?"

Antoinette looked at James and Raphael, feeling torn. She didn't want James left out, but neither did she want to offend Raphael. In the end she just smiled as Raphael and Constantin rose to leave. She, too, left before James was able to say anything.

* * *

The day after Raphael left, James arrived at the gallery, having decided that now was the time to make amends. He needed to clear the air, otherwise, things would just get even worse. Antoinette was out.

"She's only nipped out," said Eleanor. "She'll be back soon. Haven't seen you around much lately, James. You must have been busy at work. Antoinette has really missed you – there is so much to do here."

This made James feel even worse, but he made his way up to the office to wait for Antoinette. Deep in thought, looking out of the window, he didn't hear her come in.

"So, you've decided to come back then," she said curtly.

"Leave it Annie. I've done my best. I'm sorry, but I just don't like him, and I can barely face being here when he is around."

"*He* has a name, James – it's Raphael. What is wrong with you? Childish! Yes, that's what it is, childish. This is our future. You don't have to like him, but you are supposed to be a professional man, so act like one. You need to work with him. Honestly, I cannot be a referee between you. If I didn't know any better, I'd say you were jealous."

James flinched at her words. She had never spoken to him like this, but, in truth, he realised that he was indeed jealous.

"Look," he said, "you can look after things here, the exhibition will go ahead, you'll organise it all wonderfully. You don't need me, and Raphael certainly doesn't want me around."

"Suit yourself then." An uncomfortable silence ensued and then James turned and left. Antoinette turned towards the window, didn't try to stop him, and watched him walk along the wharf, his shoulders slumped.

"Damn!" she exclaimed a moment later. "That went well. Oh, James, I don't want it to be like this." Yet she knew that as long as Raphael and the exhibition remained, James' feelings would take second place. Never had there been such bad feeling between them, and she feared that things might never be the same again. "How could I say all those things?" she said and was filled with remorse.

* * *

James' dislike for Raphael festered. Yes, he really was smug, smarmy, insufferably full of himself, and James truly couldn't understand how Antoinette could be so enamoured of such a creep. Yet she was – so was it he himself who was finding it impossible to think rationally? Then there was Constantin, who seemed to be genuine, kind and thoughtful. Surely he wouldn't work for Raphael if he really was as shifty as he seemed? James mulled over all these thoughts as he walked home, and deep down he realised he wasn't totally in the wrong in his assessments: behind the façade was Raphael really all that he seemed?

* * *

With Raphael back in London, the gallery returned to a semblance of normality. The early spring exhibition had been taken down, and Antoinette smiled when she realised it had done really quite well, much of its success due to the wealthy cruise passengers who didn't seem to mind how much they spent. They patronised the cafe too, which was great. Now it was time to think about the next exhibition, and yet she was lacking the much-needed enthusiasm and commitment. She kept finding excuses to go somewhere or do something else, even though she knew it wasn't good enough. Everything seemed flat after Raphael left and, although Constantin kept in touch, it wasn't the same. What was more disconcerting was just how much she was missing James. She realised how much he contributed to the gallery, not just financially, but with ideas that helped keep her motivated. They had always worked well together, were comfortable in each other's company and had never disagreed about anything – until now. Eleanor interrupted her thoughts when she appeared in the office.

"Everything OK?" Antoinette asked her.

"Yes, fine. I was just going to get a sandwich and some fresh air and wondered if you wanted anything?"

"No, no, I'm fine. I'm not very hungry but thank you for asking."

Eleanor didn't think she seemed fine; Antoinette's eyes had a listless, faraway look and Eleanor thought she looked tired. Normally, Antoinette was bright and cheerful, enjoying her work.

"Antoinette, are you alright? You don't seem your usual self. Is there anything I can do?"

"Not really. Work just seems a bit heavy-going at present."

"I know it isn't for me to say, but maybe it's because James isn't here. I miss him and you must too." Eleanor realised she was right, as Antoinette went into full flow.

"I can't believe we argued like we did, but he is so unreasonable. I just don't know what's wrong with him. He's usually so professional."

Eleanor rolled her eyes and said to herself 'everyone but you can see how much James loves you. How can you be so blind? He wants to protect you.' She felt sorry for James. Like him, she found herself disliking Raphael, although Constantin was so handsome, and thinking of him made her feel weak at the knees.

"I don't need his sulks, Eleanor."

"But Annie, can't you understand that when he sees Raphael flaunting himself at you, he doesn't want you to get hurt?"

Antoinette knew that James was deeply upset, but both were stubborn and she wasn't going to be the one to capitulate. "I don't know what to do. I desperately need for Madrigal to be a success and I need James here to help."

"We do need him here, Antoinette!" said a frustrated Eleanor. "It may not be right for me to say this, but for goodness' sake, give him a ring; because if you don't, I don't think he will."

Chapter Three

Eleanor was right, Antoinette admitted to herself, and before she had the chance to change her mind, she rang James. "James," she whispered, "are we still friends? What has happened between us? Please don't be like this. I need you, James, I really do. I need you to help me. Madrigal is such a hugely important thing. I'll help you deal with Raphael; I promise. Are you there, James? You aren't saying anything."

"I'm here, Antoinette," he said, with deep emotion in his voice. "Are you still mad with me?"

"I can't ever really be mad with you," she replied softly. "I'm so sorry, please come back to the gallery – I need you."

"Antoinette, you know I will." James felt his heart warmed.

***

True to his word, James arrived at the gallery next morning. They hugged one another and Eleanor, sneaking a look, grinned, happy that she had helped bring about the reconciliation. 'Things will be alright now,' she told herself.

"I would never leave you in the lurch," James emphasised. "I promise I will always be here when you need me."

"Thank you." Antoinette felt her eyes misting over.

"Right then," James said to lighten the mood. "What do you want me to do? No doubt you have left a long list for me."

"No, I haven't. In fact, neither of us need to worry about lists just now." She took his hand and led him downstairs. "Come on, I'm taking you for lunch to prove how much you mean to me."

"I won't argue with that; where are we going?"

"James, 'argue' is no longer a word in our vocabulary, OK? I wondered if you had been to the new seafood restaurant near the castle? I've heard it's excellent."

"I've heard that too. I'd love to give it a try."

"Let's go then."

James fervently hoped that everything would now turn out well.

Nautilus was certainly busy, and if popularity was a guide, then they hoped for something special. The setting was spectacular; a balcony leading out from the main restaurant area looked out over the harbour and the castle, and they found a perfect small table in the sunshine. A breeze was blowing off the sea, but it was a refreshing rather than a cold one. Feeling decadent, they ordered lobster, assured by the waiter it had been freshly caught that morning. While waiting for their food, they watched the yachts and other boats, and enjoyed a chilled chardonnay, which was crisp and not too dry.

"This is the life," said James, topping up their glasses. "I'm glad you chose here – it's lovely, I'm really enjoying it. Thank you." James gave Antoinette a peck on the cheek. Life suddenly seemed very sweet, and both were a little light-headed as they left the restaurant. Antoinette twisted her shoe heel on the town cobbles and James caught her before she fell.

"Where to now, ma'am?" he asked as he grabbed her arm.

"Why don't we just stroll along the promenade? You know, when you live here, you forget to do those nice, ordinary little things. It's a lovely place to stroll." They paused as they walked along, watching the boats in the marina and then an approaching liner, one of many which berthed at St Peter Port on a regular basis.

"It's a good thing they come, isn't it, at least for us? We make a good profit from the cruises; the visitors are generous and not afraid to spend money."

"Very true," agreed Antoinette. "But you know, I bet most of them will never have been to Guernsey and don't know what to expect. They are probably genuinely surprised to see such a beautiful town and a thriving marina. And, of course, although it's British, people like the unexpected French influence. I often hear them in the gallery – they love chatting to me, wanting to know more about the island's history. They can't wait to buy some souvenirs to remind them of the unexpected gem that is Guernsey."

"Yes, we do well from them and long may it last," echoed James.

"Do you fancy a coffee?" she said, and they settled into a little café with a view of the harbour. The sea air had freshened in the breeze, the seabirds were squawking, eyes peeled for an easy lunch. They both felt relaxed and at peace, enjoying an afternoon in each other's company.

"So, now that you've taken down the old exhibition, we need to plan the next, do we?" asked James, deciding it was time for a discussion about the gallery.

"We do, and to be honest, it's proving a bit difficult."

"Why's that?"

"Well, you know we invited local artists to submit their work, months ago now. I've actually only just got around to looking at them and most leave a lot to be desired. I'm worried there may not be enough quality to form the exhibition."

"That's not good. Tell you what, I'll come to the gallery tomorrow. We'll look through them together. I'm sure we can sort it out."

"That would be great – thanks, James."

"No, Antoinette, thank you for making me realise how silly I've been."

"You aren't silly, but I'm so glad you're back on board."

"So am I." James kissed her cheek.

* * *

Next day, looking at the entries, he understood her concern. "Mm, I see what you mean. They aren't very good, are they?"

"That's an understatement," said Antoinette, somewhat exasperated. James continued studying the paintings.

"Remind me Annie, is this what we've done before for this exhibition?"

"It is. We ask local artists to submit a painting, and we decide whether to exhibit it. Most are amateurs, I know."

"Amateurs, that's quite a generous word for them. It amazes me how confident some people are, thinking they are good artists. Most of these are awful."

"They are, but what are we going to do?"

"Did you set aside any decent ones?"

"A few – they're at the end of the table." She brought them over for James to see. She picked one out. "This is by Elizabeth Guerin. She's really quite good. We sold a couple of hers last year. And then there is Guy Armond and William Wright; they're new to me, but I like them. Other than that, I wouldn't choose any of the others."

"You're right," James agreed, "these are quite good, and individual too: not run of the mill and with a good use of colour. Look, why don't we just abandon all the others, and to make up the numbers we could approach these three and ask if they could give us more. I'm sure they must have some."

"Then just have an exhibition of three artists? Good idea. As long as they can supply the volume, yes, I think it could work. We don't have to have lots of different artists, do we?"

"No, of course not," agreed James. "Then next year, if this works, we can change the emphasis. They will still be Guernsey artists, but they can only exhibit by invitation. That way we won't be bombarded with all this really substandard stuff."

"Great, let's do it. You see, this proves what we already knew; we are a great team."

Their plans went well, the three artists were absolutely delighted to submit more, and when the pictures were hung it looked a lovely exhibition.

"I think we'll do well with this, James," she said as they wandered around looking at the finished product.

During the final few days, Antoinette was left alone to finalise arrangements, and she sat down with Eleanor to check everything.

"So, how are the invitations going? Have we had many replies for the opening?"

"They are coming in thick and fast, and the local papers and lifestyle magazines have also confirmed."

"That's great, Eleanor. And the buffet – did you remember to change the champagne to prosecco?"

"All done, and it has made a real difference to the overall costings. It only leaves the flower arrangements: you said you would like to do them yourself."

"That's right, I will. So, good, everything seems to be ready. Oh, what about the artists? They will be here, won't they?"

"You must be joking, Antoinette. Wild horses wouldn't keep them away. To say that they are excited would be an understatement."

"Ah, that's lovely. I suppose I should have made time to see them again before the opening. Still, I'll see them on the evening; that will have to do. Eleanor, you know I'm really looking forward to this exhibition, and yet it was so unpromising to begin with. All you need now is a large supply of red dots. I have a feeling we may sell a lot of their work."

"Fingers crossed, Antoinette. But I must say they do look very well on display; attractive, vibrant and with totally different styles. They will attract people's attention, I'm sure."

"Oh, let's hope so. I'll leave you to finalise the arrangements then, Eleanor, while I concentrate on the flowers."

Chapter Four

Preview night was as popular as James and Antoinette had hoped. It seemed guests were genuinely interested in buying pictures, not just in being seen and enjoying free food, an observation proved by the number of red dots and 'sold' stickers appearing on the exhibits. The atmosphere was relaxed and friendly, with people chatting as they wandered up and down the gallery, some going upstairs and taking their food to the balcony to take in the fresh, but lovely evening air.

James was sitting with a glass of wine, just taking it all in.

"Well, aren't you the handsome one? You look great!" Antoinette said, and he turned to look at her.

"Well, thank you, you look quite wonderful yourself." They both smiled.

It was a good evening, one they could both be proud of. James always dressed smartly, but his smart-casual outfit really suited him; blue linen trousers and shirt topped by a tailored jacket. Antoinette realised how handsome he looked – tall and slim with his large emerald eyes, perfectly matched by his outfit, his blonde hair slightly longer than usual and slightly mussed. It was a warm evening and a little sweat shone on his upper lip. Suddenly, there was a loud noise by the entrance, and what seemed like a scuffle.

"What on earth!" exclaimed Antoinette.

"It's alright, I'll go and see what's going on." James walked rapidly towards the door. "Oh, no, please no," he sighed when he realised what was happening. Raphael, followed by Constantin, burst into the room.

"I was right!" shouted Raphael. "Look – everyone is here. It looks like a lovely exhibition." By now almost the whole gallery had turned to watch. "But where is darling Antoinette? Oh, there you are, my sweet," he said as he glided towards the buffet where Antoinette had been helping herself to some food. She turned, her eyes wide.

"Raphael, what are you doing here?"

"My darling, I have come to see you and to view this excellent exhibition." He put his arms around her and gave her a passionate kiss. "You must be pleased to see me – come here and let me look at you."

"Of course I'm pleased. I'm just surprised, that's all."

"I knew how delighted you would be by my making a special journey to see you."

Everyone was staring, wondering who on earth this loud man was. James was furious. 'What on earth is he wearing?' he thought to himself, as he looked at Raphael in his pink trousers, lilac shirt and spotted waistcoat. 'He looks ridiculous, and how dare he just turn up and turn all the attention on himself.'

A wonderful evening had suddenly turned sour. Antoinette looked embarrassed, a questioning look on her face as she turned to James. But Raphael was in charge; he took her arm and walked with her around the gallery. Slowly the guests turned away from him, and back to the exhibition. Antoinette did not know what she ought to do, but at the same time she was flattered and overwhelmed that Raphael had made a special journey to see her. No-one else seemed impressed, but her eyes glittered with pleasure.

Eleanor had seen everything, and she was not impressed by Raphael and his very large ego. She watched James at the other side of the room and felt for him. How could Antoinette not realise how much he loved her? Eleanor could see the hurt in his eyes as he watched Raphael and Antoinette, who seemed not to have eyes for anyone else. Constantin, too, had seemed a little embarrassed. He stood quietly by the door, unsure what he should be doing. Eleanor was sorry for Constantin too, but more than that, she was delighted to see him on his own, looking uncomfortable. A perfect opportunity to approach this handsome man.

"Hi, Constantin," she said, as she walked over to him. "You look a little lost. Are you okay?"

"Oh, I'm fine, thank you, Eleanor. I'm just keeping an eye on Raphael."

"Does he need to be watched over?"

Constantin laughed. "No, of course not, but I'm working and I need to make sure that everything is fine with Raphael."

"I'd say he was extremely fine just now, looking at his command of Antoinette. Come on, you can relax. Come over and have some food and wine, try to enjoy yourself."

"Yes, you're right. Thank you," he said and followed Eleanor over to the buffet. She stayed close by while he helped himself, and then led him to a quiet spot, intending to find out more about this lovely man. They sat down and he seemed much more relaxed. "So, Eleanor, you are Antoinette's assistant here. Do you enjoy it?"

"Oh, I love it, and Annie is such a great boss; and she has promised me a big bonus after Raphael's exhibition."

"That's very fair. You're at university?"

"Yes, I'll be in my final year from September. The wages here help keep me afloat. Mind you, I've no idea what I'm going to do after I graduate. I don't want to leave Guernsey, but I may have to if I want to find a good job."

"And James?" Constantin added. "He seems very nice."

"Oh, Constantin, he is. He is so generous; the gallery would never have happened if it wasn't for James' investment. I do feel sorry for him though."

"You do? Why?" asked a surprised Constantin.

"Well, because of how he feels for Antoinette. He really loves her and she just can't see it. She loves him really, though; she just needs to wake up and realise it. Anyway, what about you?" Eleanor asked, trying to change the subject.

"What do you mean?" he asked.

"Tell me something about yourself. You must be very tolerant and patient to work for Raphael. How long have you been with him?"

Constantin laughed. "He isn't so bad as he seems, you know. A lot of it is for show. But I can't say I know him all that well, I've only worked for him for just over twelve months. He can be a bit of hard work sometimes."

Eleanor spluttered over her drink as he spoke, laughing. "You're telling me! But Antoinette certainly seems to have fallen under his spell. Listen, how long are you here in Guernsey?"

"Just a couple of days. Why?"

"Well, I'm being a bit forward here, but before you go back, would you like me to show you some parts of this lovely island?"

Constantin smiled, his eyes shone, and she knew he was being honest when he replied "Be as forward as you like, Eleanor; that would be lovely. I'll look forward to it."

"Great. Now I think I'd better get back, see if I need to do anything." Leaving Constantin to his buffet, Eleanor couldn't hide her wide smile as she mingled with the guests.

Not everyone was quite so happy. Outwardly, James' professional approach found him continuing to mingle and converse to encourage sales and ignoring Raphael and Antoinette. Inside, he couldn't wait to leave. He was no longer going to let Raphael cause arguments between him and Annie, but he knew he would have to keep his emotions under control until after Raphael's exhibition was over. He sincerely hoped that Raphael would suddenly lose interest in Antoinette. He didn't want her to be hurt, but at the moment he felt there was just nothing he could do.

* * *

The next day, Antoinette had agreed to show Raphael around Ca'lou island. Having checked the tides, she knew they could walk over the causeway in the morning. She picked him up at his hotel. The Castle Manor was, as its name suggested, an old manor house facing the castle, with fabulous views out to sea. He was on time, and he jumped into Antoinette's car – a convertible Mini – with enthusiasm. She had the hood down, it being a perfect day.

"This is fabulous," Raphael enthused as he leaned over to give her a kiss. "So, we can go to the island today?"

"Definitely, the causeway will soon be clear."

"Remind me, what is it called?"

"Ca'lou."

"I hope it won't be too busy."

"Me too, but I'm sure it will be okay."

After parking the car, she led Raphael across the broad stretch of beach and to the causeway. It was fully uncovered so there was no need to splash into rock pools, although the seaweed was slippery in places. It wasn't a road exactly, but simply a loose collection of rocks and pebbles, raised up above the sand. The island looked low and barren as they stepped across. At the end, there was a small pebble beach leading to a swathe of rough and tussocky grass. People had created paths by constant use over time and Antoinette and Raphael followed a rough pathway towards what had been the little monastery. Although a lovely sunny day, the island's exposed position and lack of trees meant it was almost always a breezy little place.

"Good grief!" Raphael shouted over the wind. "Is it always like this?"

"Very often, yes."

"Then why on earth did the monks settle here? It's so inhospitable."

"Well, they liked being remote, but when we get a little closer, you'll see that they found a relatively sheltered spot."

And so it proved. Ahead of them was a substantial dip in the ground; the wind blew over the top and suddenly there was a peaceful, quiet spot. The monastery, which had always remained small, nestled in its hollow, the ruins easily accessed but with few walls intact.

"Come on, let's get inside," Raphael said, as he pulled Antoinette towards the ruins. The wind suddenly quietened and the sun shone, giving them respite to catch their breath and tame their wind-blown hair. They sat on a low wall.

"There isn't much to see, is there?" Raphael complained.

"I did say there wasn't much left, but there is a well-preserved under-croft."

"Let's go and see that then," said Raphael, getting quickly to his feet, Antoinette following, pointing out the way. There were very few people around. Antoinette knew that the number of visitors depended on the changing tides. The cleared causeway in an afternoon was always more popular. These morning low tides meant fewer people. "This is quite amazing," Raphael proclaimed. "It's so well preserved compared to everywhere else."

It was a large empty space; cavern-like with its barrel-vaulted roof and bricked floor. Their voices echoed as they walked around.

"This would have been the storage area, and there would have been shelves, barrels, and water containers, not empty like now."

Raphael had walked to a far corner where there was an ante-room. "This little room has a fireplace – look!"

"No doubt to keep the cellarer warm; it must have been freezing down here."

In the opposite corner was another small room, this one closed off. Raphael hurried towards it. There was no door, but a barrier, and a sign 'Danger. Do not enter.' Raphael seemed excited.

"I wonder if I can get over and have a look, but it is very dark. I wish I had brought my torch." He tried his best to see over the barrier, but it was completely dark on the other side. Then he seemed to decide it might be quite dangerous in there.

"Don't go in, Raphael – it isn't safe and why do you want to go in?"

"Okay, you're right. Come on, let's go. I need to get back. I have so much to do. He went into an immediate sulk and sprinted towards the exit, leaving Antoinette in his wake. "Hurry, Antoinette, come on." By the time she caught up he was almost at the causeway. She was puzzled by his sudden mood change, wondering what on earth had caused him to be so sulky and bad-tempered. He waited at the causeway, however. "Come on, let's get out of this place," he said and set off towards the mainland, Antoinette finding it hard to keep up.

"Slow down, Raphael – what's wrong?"

"Nothing, I just want to get back to my hotel."

They walked the rest of the way in silence.

Back at her car Raphael said not to bother driving him back. "I'll get a taxi," he said emphatically.

"Don't be silly," countered Antoinette, but after one look at his angry expression, she said no more. Antoinette drove off, wondering what on earth she had done to offend him, but knowing that, really, she hadn't done anything. Confused and upset, she returned to the gallery, not mentioning the experience to anyone. Yet she continued to be troubled. 'What could I have done?' she thought. 'Will he cancel the exhibition? He is so temperamental, he could well do it.' Against her better judgement, she decided to call him. He had most probably gone back to the hotel. He answered straight away.

"Have I upset you, Raphael?" she said softly, before he could speak.

"Oh, my dear, of course not. I don't know what came over me out there. I suddenly felt I needed to leave. Looking back, it was so silly. I upset you, I know, and I am sorry."

"Are we still friends then?" she asked again quietly.

"Of course, of course, we will always be friends."

Feeling reassured, Antoinette slept better that night than she thought she would, yet deep down she still didn't understand what had happened, and she knew also that she really didn't know Raphael at all. Nevertheless, reconciled, she still felt drawn to him, and she desperately wanted to keep him in her life.

Chapter Five

Time was racing by, and it was time to take down the spring exhibition. Antoinette was thrilled with the result; James' idea of reducing the number of artists had been perfect. Right from the preview night, sales had been buoyant, better than she could ever have expected. Now it was time to really get to grips with 'Madrigal'. 'August may seem a long way off,' she told herself, 'but time really does fly, and we need to be organised.' She was confident all would go well and was more relaxed; it was a good feeling.

Raphael had returned to London, and it was Constantin who was in regular contact; helping with arrangements wherever he could and coming to Guernsey when he needed to. He was impressed by James and Antoinette, and had no concerns, which helped him to keep Raphael as calm and as relaxed as it was possible for Raphael to be.

"Raphael has decided which pictures he is showing at the exhibition. It will be quite minimalistic, but the main exhibit will still be 'Madrigal', and that will be the largest one by far."

"Do you know yet how he will display it?" she asked. "Will it be complicated?"

"I don't think so. But instead of hanging on a wall, it will be suspended by almost invisible wires from the ceiling, so that it appears to be hanging in mid-air. I have to say that I think he has created a very original installation. Everyone will be astounded."

"It sounds fabulous, Constantin."

"Visitors," continued Constantin, "will be able to walk around it completely, as the painting will be double sided."

Antoinette was incredibly excited and couldn't wait to tell James.

A few days later, Constantin phoned again, saying he and Raphael would be coming over the following weekend. "Raphael is concerned that he hasn't yet been to the lifeboat station," he said. "He wants to meet the crew and I think he's going to make a donation."

"But I thought he was giving the proceeds from one of his paintings."

"Yes, he is, I think that this is extra, but I'm not entirely sure. But he asked if you could arrange some publicity for him, newspapers, local TV and things. He might be generous, but he isn't entirely altruistic."

"Constantin, that is the first time I have heard a negative comment from you about Raphael," she laughed.

"Well, he is my employer, but no-one is perfect," he said and he laughed too. "Also, he wants you to check that everything is in hand – insurance, publicity and whatever."

"It already is, he knows that, but yes, I will check and I'll arrange the meeting with the lifeboat crew too."

"That's great, Antoinette. I'm looking forward to seeing you and James again. And will you to tell Eleanor that I will be in Guernsey next week?"

"I will – is something going on with you two?"

"We're just friends, that's all."

"Ah, of course, and that explains this wonderful mood of Eleanor's, does it?"

"Yes, probably. I'll see you next week."

The mystery remained unsolved, but Antoinette knew that a relationship was unfolding between Eleanor and Constantin. She couldn't blame her, he was such a lovely, kind and handsome man. Antoinette was still unsure about Raphael. He had apologised and she knew it should have been enough. He was highly strung and nervous. Yet she was excited at the thought of seeing him again. He was certainly unpredictable. Was that why she was so attracted to him?

When Antoinette met him at the airport, Raphael was gushing. "My darling, I'm so delighted to see you again," he said, his smile broad and his eyes shining. "Surely you must be glad to see me too?" Antoinette seemed a little hesitant.

"Raphael, of course I am, I'm just getting more nervous as the exhibition gets closer."

"No, don't be nervous. Everything will be fabulous, you'll see. How could it not be? My exhibitions are always brilliant. Everyone wants to see my art; they know I'm the best and most famous artist in the world." Antoinette couldn't help but smile. "That's better. Come here." He put down his overnight bag and gave her a hug. "Anyway, look at my T-shirt – how could anyone ignore it?" He showed Antoinette where, written in large letters, were the words 'Me! The best artist in the world? – probably!'

Antoinette laughed out loud. "Oh, honestly, you are incorrigible."

"Yes, I am, aren't I?"

"Now come on, let's get you to your hotel."

"Different one this time. I'm staying at the Guernsey Jewel."

"Well, lucky you! By the way, where is Constantin?"

"There was a little complication in London; he's coming on later when it's sorted."

* * *

Fortunately, it was a calm day when Raphael was expected at the Lifeboat Station. Antoinette couldn't have coped with all the complaints from him if it had been a rough sea. The skipper and some of his crew were waiting outside the Station, but the boat itself had already been launched and bobbed gently on the sea below. She was pleased to see that newspaper journalists, and even local TV had turned up, and Raphael's display was nothing short of amazing. Certainly, you couldn't miss him. His hair was partially dyed a deep purple and the rest of his outfit both matched and clashed in equal ways.

It was a perfect day and quite a crowd had gathered on the quayside.

"So, Mr Harcourt-Smythe," asked the TV reporter, as Raphael smiled broadly at the camera. "What has brought you here to our lovely island? We understand you are to hold an exhibition at La Perle gallery, but what is your connection with the lifeboat here?"

Raphael, in his usual arrogant way, replied: "Well, of course, you know I am a very famous and wealthy artist. And, you see, the lifeboat crew here were so brave and wonderful when they rescued my father in a terrible gale. I am so grateful to them, and I also knew it would be a great honour for them to meet me and receive this generous donation to the lifeboat fund.

If the skipper would like to receive it, I have a cheque for £100,000." There were gasps from the spectators, and Simon Batiste, the skipper, was equally shocked. He looked as if he was ready to faint. Nevertheless, he smiled broadly as he took the cheque from Raphael, the newspaper photographer clicking and hoping for a good picture.

"So, skipper," continued the Border TV reporter, "were you expecting such a large donation?"

"Er, no," stuttered the shocked skipper. "I had no idea Mr Harcourt-Smythe was such a famous artist, but we are indeed grateful for his very generous donation."

The smile slipped from Raphael's face. He was feeling somewhat insulted, but he soon recovered.

"Of course, I wouldn't expect a lifeboat crew to be acquainted with high art," he retaliated. "But no doubt you will all now remember this important day."

Despite the generous donation, the skipper's face was like thunder, but he said nothing. Instead, he forced a smile. "It is, of course, a memorable day, and if you are ready, Mr Harcourt-Smythe, the boat is waiting to take you out into the bay."

"Thank you, yes, I'm ready." As he walked toward the slipway he turned and waved to everyone. "I hope you will all be able to come and see my brilliant exhibition at La Perle gallery. Normally, I wouldn't contemplate an exhibition in such a small unknown gallery, but I thought it would help in giving thanks for my father's rescue. You probably can't afford the prices my paintings command, but do still come and admire. Then you won't be surprised at the millions of pounds people are prepared to pay for them."

There were gasps from the small crowd, some offended, others laughing at the ridiculous confidence of this man they had never heard of. As the boat sailed out, he waved energetically, like the celebrity he thought he was. Simon Batiste was less than impressed with their guest, but he remained courteous. He said nothing, but neither he nor his crew could remember anything about Raphael's father being rescued by them. It was either a long time ago, or perhaps he had the wrong island. It didn't matter, because the money was extremely welcome. Oblivious, Raphael was enjoying the fresh air and he relaxed as they hugged the Guernsey coast. He called the skipper over, his arrogance gone.

"That little island," he asked. "Is it Ca'lou?"

"Yes, that's right. Do you know it?"

"I walked out to it recently. Very blustery but interesting. I looked around the ruined monastery there – quite extraordinary that the monks could live in such a spot. But tell me, what is the other landmark at the other end of the island? I never managed to get there."

"Oh, it's nothing more than one of our many German bunkers, found all over this island of ours. Blots on the landscape, we call them."

"Oh, how horrid. So, have these bunkers all been blocked off? I can't imagine anyone wanting to visit them."

"Actually," he replied, "many are still open and some relics of our German occupation are now tourist attractions; the underground German hospital being possibly the most visited. In terms of the bunkers, though, many are quite large but very spooky inside."

"Can you get inside this one on Ca'lou?" Raphael asked.

"I believe you can but as it's on a little island and a little isolated, it's not really on the tourist trail. It's probably open, but I wouldn't like to go in there. They say some strange things happen."

"You mean ghosts and things?"

"Aye, something like that," the skipper answered enigmatically.

"How interesting. What a strange thing, to have had the German army here."

"Definitely strange, Mr Harcourt-Smythe, and horrible, really horrible."

"Indeed, yes," Raphael replied. "And thank you for telling me."

"No problem." The skipper wondered about this artist, who suddenly seemed like a totally different person.

Raphael found himself deep in thought and was quiet all the way back to St Peter Port.

* * *

Next day Raphael was in an expansive, even happy, mood.

"I knew all was well with the arrangements. Constantin was positive about them, but I did want to check myself and, of course, I really wanted to see you, my darling." Antoinette blushed. "I love these invitations, Antoinette, and so many people, even from the mainland and France, have already confirmed they will come. But then, of course, I knew they would; they like to be seen in all the right places. You really have done marvellously; I knew from the beginning I could trust you." They sat on the balcony looking out over the sea, sparkling in the sun. "Do you always have such great weather here?"

"Not always, but often – it's quite continental at this time of year."

"You're right, it feels quite French today. How far away are you from France?"

"Well, Alderney is the closest of the Channel Islands to the French coast, but we aren't that far, although going by yacht isn't easy because there are some difficult tides."

"But there are so many yachts out here," and Raphael pointed to the large number, some close and others, clearly heading away from Guernsey. "So will those farthest away be going to France?"

"Probably, but most are locals and know these seas, so they are used to it. It isn't a place for novice yachties, though."

"So those less expert could charter boats if they wanted?"

"Yes, there are lots of charter yachts. You can see them in the harbour at St Peter Port. You aren't thinking of taking up sailing, are you?"

"Why not?" Antoinette looked at him wide-eyed. "Only joking, Antoinette, but maybe in the future. It seems a lovely hobby."

"Yes, and expensive, but then I suppose you can afford it."

"No, it isn't the cost or snob value, it's just a great way to relax and get away from it all."

"Not so relaxing in choppy waters, which are quite frequent here. My father has a nice yacht, though. I'm sure he would take you out if you asked."

"You are wonderful, do you know that?" He took her hand, looked deep into her eyes and kissed her. "Now," Raphael continued, "the next important thing is to bring over my paintings."

Antoinette had only half listened. She was in something of a reverie after Raphael's kiss. "Sorry, what did you say, Raphael?"

He smiled almost indulgently. "I said the next job is to transport my paintings to Guernsey."

"Of course! Do you want me to do it?"

"No, no, sweetheart. I'll take care of it all. I'll send them by container, I'm used to it. But, Antoinette, I need to be sure that the insurance is in place, prior to the exhibition."

"I told you Raphael, it's already arranged. If you let me know when the paintings are due to arrive, I'll sort it out. There is no need to worry."

"I'm not worried, just concerned that everything is in place. If anything happens to my paintings in transit, I need to know the insurance will cover it."

"I understand, Raphael, you can trust me." She squeezed his hand.

"I know, I do trust you." He looked into her eyes and saw that there was more than just trust in them.

Chapter Six

James had managed to avoid Raphael most of the time and been happy to liaise with Constantin. Now that preparations were well under way, he didn't need to go into the gallery quite so often either. Overall, he was feeling more relaxed, and decided to update Gabriel about the exhibition. He was looking forward to a good chat and a few drinks. Gabriel had been married to Laura for two years and she was now pregnant. He knew they were both looking forward to the baby's arrival, but had chosen not to know if it was a boy or a girl. It was a beautiful evening and they settled into a little trattoria close to the harbour in St Peter Port. Little Giovanni's was a popular spot, looking out as it did across the harbour where the yachts lined up and their ropes slapped against the masts. The food competed well with the atmosphere, conversation from customers getting louder as the evening wore on and prosecco was consumed. James and Gabriel, as they sat on the outside terrace, enjoyed a meal of pasta and a dry white wine, followed by ice cream and liqueur.

"It's great to get out and relax," said James, "and a change from just a couple of pints at the pub. It takes the pressure from the exhibition."

"Is it that bad?"

"Not really, I suppose, and things are coming together now. Anyway, what have you been up to? How's Laura?"

"Fed up. She's getting really big now and is uncomfortable, especially in bed."

"How much longer has she to go now?"

"About three months. We've been sorting out a nursery, so that takes her mind off things. It's getting exciting, James, but a bit frightening too."

"You still don't know whether it's a girl or a boy?"

"No, it'll be a lovely surprise, and lemon for the nursery colour covers both options. How are things at the gallery? Are you getting on with the people there now?"

"I don't see much of Raphael. I go to the gallery when he isn't there. Constantin is great to work with, though."

"Do you like him any better now?" asked Gabriel, meaning Raphael.

"You must be joking! I can't stand him; he's still an ignorant snob as far as I'm concerned. Antoinette says there is a softer side to him but I can't see it. However, I don't want to jeopardise the exhibition, so I just keep out of the way. I worry about Annie though; I really don't want her to get hurt."

Just then there was movement, and some people emerged from the restaurant on to the terrace.

"I'm glad it wasn't all a hoax, James – you both deserve to do well. Annie works so hard."

James shushed Gabriel as he heard voices across the terrace.

"What?" queried Gabriel.

"Shh, listen, it's Raphael and Constantin, his agent. They must have been inside while we were out here." James turned away so Raphael wouldn't see him, even though the dimly lit terrace helped keep him from view. Then he tried to listen to what they were saying.

"Are you sure they'll be there now, Constantin?"

"Yes, come on or we'll miss them."

"Don't hassle me, I'm coming!" he said and they both left the restaurant hurriedly.

James, having heard, thought them quite furtive and he was intrigued. 'What are they up to?' he thought to himself. But they had left before he could hear more.

"Wait here, Gabriel, I won't be long."

"Where are you going?"

"Following them."

"Who?"

"That was Raphael and Constantin. I want to find out what they are up to."

"They might not be up to anything, James. Sit down, leave it."

49

But James couldn't leave it. "No, I'm going to follow them. I don't trust them, Gabriel."

And before any more could be said, James went out into the night, and followed Raphael and Constantin, who appeared to be crossing the road to the Marina.

'Why on earth would they be going to the Marina at this time of night? They're up to something, but what?' He followed close behind, as they headed to one of the jetties and then walked along a pontoon, where they stopped.

James was confused, and stayed in the dark, as he wondered what was going on. Then, from below the pontoon, two men climbed up the ladder and joined Raphael and Constantin. There were hushed voices but James heard Raphael's voice.

"So, can you do it?"

"Course we can, no problem."

"How much?" …but then a breeze caught their voices and James didn't hear any more. He quickly made his way back to the trattoria.

"What was that all about?" asked a frustrated Gabriel.

"I don't know, but why hang around the marina so furtively at this time of night, and who were they talking to?"

"So that was the famous Raphael. He is rather flamboyant, isn't he?"

"That's not the half of it. He's arrogant, supercilious and loud."

"Oh, you really like him then!" said Gabriel, and they both laughed.

Despite the laughter, though, James pondered on what he had seen. Something wasn't quite right, but he didn't know what or why.

* * *

Constantin, too, was somewhat flummoxed by his employer's actions. On the way back to their hotel he couldn't help but question Raphael.

"Why did we have to meet them like that, in the dark. You only wanted to go to Ca'lou – what's the problem?"

"I want to go when the tide is in, so no-one else will be there. I need some time to myself. They have agreed to take me."

"But why so furtive, Raphael? I don't understand it."

"It isn't for you to question what I do. I pay you to do as you are told. I know what I'm doing. So, do you want to come out to the island and see inside the bunker?"

"I don't want to but seeing it's so important to you, then of course, I will."

"Thank you. That's settled then. You will know my plans soon enough."

On that enigmatic note, Constantin decided to ask no more questions.

* * *

Very early the next day, before flying back to London, Raphael and Constantin were walking along the beach which led to Ca'lou, but the tide was in and little sand was exposed. Ca'lou island was completely cut off. The owner of a little beach café was getting everything ready for the day ahead. She saw two men hanging around, clearly waiting for something. Then a boat appeared, putt-putting, then cutting its engine as it approached the beach.

"This was a really good idea, Con – no-one will be going to Ca'lou so early and we'll have this lovely tiny island to ourselves."

Constantin was generally a patient man; no-one who worked for Raphael could be otherwise. But he was sorely tested this morning. He couldn't understand why Raphael was so determined to get to the island. He had told Constantin that he didn't want anyone else there as he was so famous, and he didn't want to be recognised, because he needed time alone. Yet this attitude didn't gel with his usual wish to be admired and feted. Raphael was moody and sometimes difficult, but could also be unpredictable, and he was always hyper before an exhibition. Constantin sighed and put this strange expedition down to Raphael's angst and knew he would just have to go along with it, and calm him down if he could. There was no jetty so they had to wade from the beach out to the boat, which was idling just off shore. They waded out a little way, and climbed into the boat where the two men were waiting to take them to Ca'lou. As the boat chugged away, the woman in the beach hut looked out and saw the boat moving away. 'They must have gone fishing,' she thought, 'but it isn't where fishermen usually leave from.'

It was still early, but it promised to be another lovely day, although there was freshness in the light breeze. Seabirds circled, screeching and screaming, ready to follow the boat, hoping for fish scraps to be thrown overboard.

"Can't think why you want to go to the island so early," the boatman said.

"Well, it's a good time when it's quiet to watch the birds, and maybe catch sight of some seals bobbing, or even resting on the island rocks off-shore, will it not?" Raphael said.

"Oh, it will be quiet certainly."

"And we also want to look around the bunker. With no-one else around we'll get a much better feel for the atmosphere."

"You'll certainly get that," answered the boatman who was handling the tiller. "I guarantee you won't stay in there long."

Constantin was still puzzled at what was going on in Raphael's mind. He couldn't think of a time when he had been remotely interested in looking at birds and seals. He sighed, knowing that Raphael needed to get whatever it was out of his system.

It was a only short sail, no more than a few minutes, and they were already approaching the island. It looked serene in the early morning light.

"You're sure the bunker will be open?" asked Raphael.

"Definitely. It's never locked."

The boat approached a little shingly beach, and dropped anchor slightly off-shore, so they had to splash and wade ashore.

"Couldn't you get any nearer?" Raphael shouted. "I'm wet through."

"Sorry about that," he replied, and Constantin could see that he wasn't sorry at all.

"Come back in two hours," Raphael ordered, now in a real sulk.

"We will." Off the little boat went, leaving Raphael and Constantin rather bedraggled amongst the tussocky grass.

"I'm absolutely soaked," Raphael moaned.

"You'll soon dry, the sun will be warm."

Raphael was not comforted by Constantin's words and walked off, leaving him in his wake. At the other end of the island from the old monastery, there couldn't have been a greater contrast. Far from ruined, the bunker's concrete walls rose up on a little promontory, ugly and forbidding. 'Bunker' seemed almost a totally inappropriate word to describe it, as it wasn't underground and stood, high and solid, dominating its surroundings. As far as Raphael could see, there were no windows, but the door was easy to see. Arriving first, Raphael waited for Constantin. He looked up at the monstrosity in front of him, a mass of concrete towering overhead. It was hard to believe it had been built in World War Two. It was substantial, with no wear or damage. Overall, it was a hideous glowering reminder of the Occupation. Raphael felt himself shiver, it was not somewhere you would choose to inhabit, yet the Germans did, along with many more across the Channel Islands.

"Not very inviting, is it?" commented Constantin when he arrived.

"No, it's quite monstrous, but I still want to see inside."

"I'll let you go first then, Raphael."

Raphael gave an angry frown but headed to the door. It was an old, heavy wooden door, eroded over the years but still sturdy. Constantin thought it incongruous against the stark, still white, concrete; the door wasn't original. When Raphael pushed, it opened easily enough, squeaking slightly on its rusty hinges. They knew the bunker was empty, but still they crept in slowly. As expected, it was totally dark, and smelled musty and dank, though Raphael was relieved that the floor itself was dry in spite of being covered in years of grime and rubbish. A few yards further in, both took out their torches and crunched along the detritus on the floor. Then suddenly there was an intense fluttering and both felt their heads brushed by what seemed like hundreds of tiny silent wings. Raphael screamed and Constantin instinctively raised his hands to protect his head.

"It's alright, Raphy, it's just bats."

"Just bats?" Raphael replied in a scared, high-pitched voice. "I nearly died of fright."

"They've all gone now, it's OK," Constantin reassured him. Raphael let out a deep grunt. "This place is horrible," said Constantin. "Are you sure you still want to look around?"

"Of course! I'm alright now. Come on, let's see the rest."

The darkness seemed dense, almost smothering, and only their torches gave a slight view of what was around them. Then, a little further in, light seemed to seep in from another area and Raphael headed towards it. In front of them was a large opening, sea air rushing in through it.

"This must be the lookout post. See, Constantin, there's a ledge to stand the guns on, and I think there's another one abutting the window." Raphael climbed up and was faced with a wonderful view. "Good grief, Con. No wonder they built it here. Take a look."

Being taller, Constantin had no trouble looking out. "This ledge must have been the gun platform, and they would have seen anything coming from miles around, by sea or air. It's horrible to think of Germans here, so close to the UK. I simply can't imagine how it must have been for the people here to live with the Occupation. Come on, if you've seen enough, I certainly have," he said but as he turned, he realised that Raphael had wandered off.

Raphael flashed his torch towards Constantin.

"I'm just over here. There are so many different small rooms. Did the Germans actually live in here, do you think?"

"I've no idea, but I'd hate to think I'd have to."

"Yes, me too." They were back together. "Look at this tiny room – what was this for, I wonder?"

"Probably lavatories, it smells absolutely terrible. Come on, Raphy, you must have seen enough. Let's get out of here."

"Okay, you're right, come on."

They almost ran back to the entrance, being careful not to trip or slip. Then they were out in the sunshine, a slight breeze ruffling their hair, the raucous gulls almost a reassuring noise. They sat down on some tussocky grass, both relieved to be out of the place.

Constantin shivered. "No wonder no-one goes in there, Raphy."

"It isn't just the dark and cold, or even the dankness and damp, there's something else isn't there? Hard to describe, though," agreed Raphael.

"It's as if an atmosphere was left, after the Germans had gone. As if part of whatever happened here was left behind. You can almost taste the fear and emotions, almost as if they were still here."

"People are right to say it is haunted."

Both lapsed into their own thoughts, and Raphael's thoughts were dark indeed. They waited impatiently for the boat to take them back. It sailed into a slightly different site on the island, more rocky than sandy. They stepped aboard the slightly rocking boat, almost oblivious to the movement, but quickly aware when Constantin seemed to lose his balance and stumbled on board. They were barely settled in the boat when it lurched forward and set off at a fair old pace for a small boat.

"We said it wasn't very nice in there, didn't we?" the boatman said. "We were right, weren't we?"

"Yes, you certainly were," agreed Raphael, and he glanced back to see the bunker fade into the distance; the concrete stark and forbidding against the green grass surrounding it. A shiver ran down his spine and, looking at Constantin, he seemed to be feeling the same way. They were cold and wet, but both knew that wasn't what had caused them to shiver. Back on Guernsey's mainland, and despite the still early hour, Raphael suggested a fortifying drink, and Constantin agreed wholeheartedly. Later the same day, they both flew back to London.

Chapter Seven

Later in the week, Antoinette heard from Constantin that Raphael's paintings were in the process of being packed and dispatched to a container in Portsmouth. She felt a fluttering in her stomach: it now felt so real.

"So, when can I expect them?"

"Probably next Saturday, that will still give us lots of time to unpack and display them. Oh, and no surprise, he wants to know how the invitations are going."

"Tell him 'great', Constantin – absolutely no need to worry. The design itself is spectacular and is grabbing attention. There are some very famous names who've said they'll come. It's quite amazing really that all these people are prepared to leave their London hub and come over to Guernsey."

"They'll go where they are noticed, Antoinette. Don't you worry about that, they will certainly come. Which reminds me, how is the publicity going?"

"Not bad so far, but I shall need to work on magazines and TV from further afield than Guernsey. I've also had some discussions with 'Front Row' on Radio 4, as well as the arts reviewers for the national papers. I'm hoping they'll love the idea of coming over to Guernsey for a couple of days and sending back a review. What do you think about Raphael doing an individual interview?"

Constantin laughed. "Well, it's a good idea, but we both know what he's like. If he's temperamental on the day, I hate to think how it would go. Why don't you arrange it so that the media interview you and James at La Perle. After all, it's such a scoop for you two – why not have some free publicity?"

"That's a good idea, but will Raphael be upset, not to be in the limelight?"

"Possibly, but leave it with me. I'll work on him."

"Thanks, Constantin, I appreciate it."

* * *

Antoinette thought she heard the gallery door open and hoped it would be James; she needed to tell him about the arrival of the paintings. She slipped out of the office and shouted down the stairs.

"Is that you, James?"

"Yes, it's me, Annie. Hi, everything okay?"

"Yes, you are just the person I want to see."

"OK, coming up."

Antoinette filled the kettle so they could relax while updating each other.

"So, his paintings are packed and ready to be sent."

"Yes, James." They looked at each other. "It's a bit scary, isn't it? It all seems so very real. It wasn't a fairy tale after all. Oh, I feel so nervous!"

He took her hand. He thought she was looking tired and strained but said nothing except to reassure her. "Annie, everything will be fine, you know it will."

"It isn't even about the money any more. I just want it all to go well, and for his paintings to sell. I'm more concerned about our reputation than anything."

James pulled her from the chair. "Come on, we need more than that coffee," he said and led her downstairs. "You need a break Annie – you are stressed."

"Where are we going?"

"Not sure, but you need to get out of here for a while."

"But Eleanor isn't in today. I just can't leave the gallery."

"Of course you can. Are you expecting anyone?"

"No, but…"

"No buts."

They emerged into the sunshine, James locking the gallery door as they left. His convertible Mercedes was parked close by, and before she could think clearly, James had whisked her away. It was a small island, but there was always a little corner somewhere that was quiet and peaceful. With the hood down, the wind catching at her hair, Antoinette let herself relax as James drove down the little lanes, lush and green, with hedgerows full of wild flowers.

"This is great, James, just what I needed. Everywhere is looking beautiful." Ahead and around each bend, there was a sudden view of the sea, shimmering blue and green in the sun. There were so many beaches, and despite the many visitors, locals could always find an uncrowded beach away from the popular spots. Coming to the end of the road, James slowed down and drove straight onto the beach. Fern Beach was no more than a small cove, sheltered by overhanging cliffs. It was warm, and the sea welcoming, small waves rippling gently and lapping onto the beach. The sand was dotted with rock pools, and wading birds wandered up and down, looking and digging for tasty morsels under the sand. They both got out. Antoinette stretched and breathed deeply at the salty air. Meanwhile, James opened the boot and brought out a rug.

"Shall we sit over there?" he suggested, "sheltered by the overhanging rock?"

"Oh, yes," agreed Antoinette.

"You make your way over and I'll join you. Here, take the blanket with you."

It didn't take long for Annie to spread the blanket and sit down, from where she watched a group of oyster catchers parading up and down the sand. James followed shortly afterwards. Antoinette watched him. "What have you got there?" she asked.

"Oh, this? Just a nice bottle of freshly chilled white wine. I wasn't a boy scout for nothing: be prepared and all that."

"How come you just happen to have wine and glasses with you? I'm beginning to think some plotting has been going on here."

"Not at all. To be honest I'd just been shopping before I got to the gallery, and for some reason I always have some glasses in the car. You just never know when they might come in useful."

"Honestly, James. Come on then – aren't you going to open it?"

"I sure am." He poured out two glasses and then sat down to join Antoinette. The overhang of rock was a perfect backrest, if a little lumpy and hard. Antoinette closed her eyes as she sipped the wine.

"This is perfect. Why don't we do this more often?"

"I suppose because we both lead such busy lives. You're right though, we should take more time out – it's restorative."

They were both quiet, each with their own thoughts. Antoinette turned her face to the sun, relaxed, feeling she could be miles away from her busy life. James' thoughts were somewhat different. He looked at Antoinette, her face tranquil and at peace, and said to himself 'I love you, Annie. I really hope all our efforts will prove worthwhile; I do so want you to be happy.' He topped up Antoinette's glass, being more careful with his own. Antoinette opened her eyes and looked at him. He looked into her eyes – a beautiful colour, so dark a blue they were almost violet – and at her hair, blowing in the slight breeze, becoming lighter as summer progressed. She smiled.

"What are you thinking? You look so serious?"

"Not serious, just thinking how lucky we are, and praying it will continue."

"I'm sure it will." She took his hand, kissed it and then lay down on the blanket. Within minutes she was asleep and James took the glass from her without wakening her. He looked to the future, to see the success of the exhibition, and the hope that Antoinette would remain in his life.

* * *

Everything was coming together, even though Raphael seemed to constantly change his mind about food. But nothing fazed Antoinette.

"He wants lobster, crab and caviar now. And the most expensive champagne!" she moaned one day to Eleanor. "But it's his exhibition, and whatever he wants, that's alright with me. As long as everything is alright on the night, I don't care."

"That's the attitude," said Eleanor supportively. "Whatever he wants, we can do it, and you know it will be worth it."

"I do hope so, my dear Eleanor."

"Listen, Annie, I've been wanting to ask you something."

"Ooh, that sounds ominous!"

"No, not at all, and it's silly really in the scheme of things, but I don't know what to wear for the big event."

Antoinette laughed, but in a kindly way. "Why are you so worried?"

"Because there will be so many rich and famous people here, all dressed in their designer clothes, trying to compete with one another. To be honest, Annie, I just don't have the money to buy anything expensive."

"Eleanor, don't fret about that. You'll be more stylish and beautiful than most of the guests."

"But I'll still be in my 'off-the-peg' clothes. I'm afraid people will point and laugh at me." She seemed terribly concerned.

Antoinette spoke quite softly to her. "I wouldn't let that happen to you. Don't forget I'm also poor compared to so many of our guests. We'll both look fabulous, really, we will. Tell you what – I will buy you a dress. I want you to look stunning too."

"I can't let you do that."

"Yes, you can," Antoinette insisted. "No argument. I really value the work you do here. We are a team, and it's the least I can do, especially if it makes you feel more on a level with our rich-list visitors. I suspect, though, that there might be another reason you perhaps want to look your best."

Eleanor's eyes widened in surprise. "I don't know what you mean," she replied coyly.

"Oh, I think you do. It may have something to do with a man called Constantin."

Eleanor blushed: of course Antoinette was right. "I really like him, Annie. He's such a lovely person; I've never met anyone like him before. Am I being silly, do you think?"

"No, not at all. I also think he is very lovely, and I'm sure he will love you in whatever you wear. To make sure though, I *will* buy you that special dress."

"Thank you, Annie. I couldn't ever wish for an employer as good and kind as you."

Now Antoinette felt herself blush. "Thank you, Eleanor, I appreciate that so much."

* * *

It would take very little effort for Antoinette's family to attend the preview. Not so for James, whose family was more widely spread across the English mainland. He spoke regularly to them, just as he was doing today.

"Hello, darling," his mother Julia enthused. "Hope all is well there; we can't wait to see you, and of course we're both really excited about the preview."

"That's great Mum. When do you expect to arrive, and do I need to pick you up?"

"No, no, sweetheart. Your Dad and I are driving down from here to Poole and taking the ferry across. I think it will be mid-afternoon on Wednesday, and we'll get a taxi. The hotel is close by, I think. The Meribel, isn't it?"

"Yes, it's very easy to get to from the port, and it's a lovely hotel. But are you sure you don't need me?"

"Don't be silly, you've enough to do, and we can meet up later."

"Antoinette and I have arranged a meal for us all. Her parents want to meet you and Dad again; it seems ages since they saw you."

"That would be lovely. What a surprise! I'm so excited James. I just can't wait!"

"Mum, what about Georgia and Oliver? Have they sorted out their travel arrangements?"

"Oh yes, darling, but they have decided to fly in from Gatwick. Now, I think they will need you to meet them."

"That's no problem. Ask them to let me know what time the plane lands. They are bringing Luca too, though, aren't they? I can't wait to see my nephew."

"I'm not sure, James; they're a bit worried he might be disruptive. I think Oliver's mum has said she will look after him, but I know Georgia would rather bring him. He's only little – would he be too boisterous, do you think?"

"No, let him come. They'll only be worrying all the time otherwise."

"Great, I'll tell her, she'll be relieved."

"OK Mum, I need to go now, but I'll see you next week."

"Bye then, darling. Love you!"

"Love you too, Mum."

* * *

Julia was overjoyed about going to Guernsey, more about seeing James than the exhibition if she was honest. Nevertheless, she couldn't wait to meet all the famous people who James said would be coming to the gallery. She hadn't heard of Raphael but knew this was all really important to James and Antoinette. All the same she missed him. He was happy in Guernsey, she knew that. If only he and Antoinette could sort out their relationship. What was wrong with Antoinette? She must know how much he loves her. I do hope all the guests are not too snobbish, she thought, and her mind wandered back to the preview night. What am I going to wear and, more important, how am I going to get Johnny into a suit?

* * *

The rest of the week whizzed by. James had been down to the container port to check the paintings had been loaded. There would be no problem, they said; the arrival would definitely be on Saturday. Relieved, he drove back to La Perle. Antoinette was growing more anxious by the day and he tried to be with her as often as possible. She was waiting for him and he knew immediately that something was wrong.

"The string quartet, James – one of them has had a fall and broken her arm. It's a disaster! What are we going to do?"

"Can't they be a trio instead?" James replied.

"This is not a joke, James, please."

"I wasn't joking, honestly," But one look at her face and he knew she was really wound up.

He threw up his hands. "OK, I'm sorry, so come on, let's see what we can do." He ushered her into the office for details.

"Remind me, who are they and who is the leader?"

"Honestly, James, you should know."

"Yes, probably I should. But you booked them, and just at the moment I can't bring them to mind," he reminded her calmly.

"It's the Southampton Strings Consort and the leader is Tom Corrigan. I've got his number here on my phone."

"Please calm down, Annie. Sit down, I'll sort it."

"Oh, hello. Is that Mr. Corrigan?" James asked as the call was answered almost immediately.

"I'm James Kerrissey, a partner at La Perle gallery on Guernsey. I believe we have a problem with your booking for our exhibition preview?"

"Sorry, Mr Kerrisey, I was just about to ring Ms Duchenne back. I've sorted it – I've managed to find a replacement, so it's not a problem now. I'll see you next Friday."

"Thank you, that's great."

"What's great, James?" Annie asked, a slight panic in her voice.

"Relax, he's found someone else. They have a lot of contacts, these people. They can usually manage to find someone to step in at the last minute."

"Thank goodness. I was worried what Raphael would say if they didn't arrive."

"Please stop worrying about what Raphael will think. We have done our best and everything will be fine. Look at me," said James. Antoinette looked up. "Repeat after me, everything will be fine." Then Antoinette laughed and the strain left her face, although she still looked tired.

* * *

Saturday dawned dull and grey and didn't improve as the morning progressed. Raphael and Constantin, staying at the Olive Tree a few miles from St Peter Port, had hired a car. James and Antoinette had agreed to meet them at the port. Constantin was driving. Raphael was more edgy than usual – if that were possible. A few spots of rain hit the windscreen bringing Raphael into full panic mode.

"It mustn't rain, it mustn't, Constantin! I can't risk any of my paintings getting wet, the idea is inconceivable."

"It's only a few spots," comforted Constantin. "I really don't think it's going to rain properly." Constantin himself was feeling Raphael's stress. 'It's like looking after a baby,' he said to himself. Then, as they approached St Peter Port, blue sky began to appear and a weak sun filtered through the remaining cloud.

"See, I told you, Raphy – look, it's brightening up."

"Good job too," he replied sulkily.

* * *

Porters allowed them through the barriers when they explained their business, and they drove along the dockside to where the porters had explained was the container area. They immediately saw Antoinette and James, both wrapped up against the morning chill. The dock was an exposed, windy spot at the best of times. Raphael ran straight up to Antoinette and hugged her.

"My darling, I couldn't wait to see you," and then gave her a passionate kiss. James turned away, and Antoinette, too, was embarrassed.

"So, today's the day, Raphael," she said, trying to calm James' obviously ruffled feathers.

But James had told himself that he was not going to rise to anything Raphael said or did, and the fact that he hadn't yet welcomed James did not faze him. With a big smile James spoke. "Good to see you, Raphael," he said and held out his hand. Reluctantly, Raphael had no alternative than to shake it. "And Constantin, great to see you again," and both men smiled, happy and comfortable in each other's company.

Antoinette immediately concealed her wide-eyed look on seeing James' friendly approach to Raphael.

"So, we'd better go and collect my precious paintings. Do we know where to go?" Raphael asked.

"I checked earlier," said James. "They have arrived safely and have been unloaded. Come on, I know where they are." He set off at a pace.

"Thank you, James." Raphael replied.

Shocked that Raphael had personally addressed him, James smiled, knowing that finally things were going smoothly. Constantin and Antoinette, however, walking behind, offered each other a confused look, both knowing their thoughts without speaking. Antoinette shrugged and Constantin raised his eyebrows, both thinking that everything boded well. Antoinette had ordered a specialist company to load and transport the paintings to the gallery. They were a pristine and expert service that Antoinette had used before. She knew they would arrive safely at La Perle where Eleanor was waiting.

Chapter Eight

The paintings were well packed and had travelled well. The couriers had no problem loading the precious cargo, and everyone agreed to meet at La Perle to help unload.

"I'll be glad to get off this dock. I can't understand why it is so chilly," complained Antoinette as they walked quickly back to their car. Raphael and Constantin were already out of sight as they had hurriedly followed the van across St Peter Port. James and Antoinette arrived back at the gallery to find Raphael supervising the unloading. Constantin just looked on, embarrassed.

"Be careful, be careful, these are my precious paintings. They're worth millions."

The couriers were trying to stay polite. "It's alright sir, we're used to this, we're experts. Nothing will happen to them."

"Yes, but they aren't yours, are they? You don't care about them."

"Of course, we do, sir, that's what we're paid for."

Finally, all were safely unloaded and securely stored in the gallery. Raphael never acknowledged the couriers, and started minutely studying his packages to ensure all was well. It was left to Antoinette and James to show the drivers to the door and thank them for their care and patience. Constantin joined them, looking as if he wanted to be somewhere else.

"Sorry," said Antoinette.

"No problem, Ms Duchenne, we're used to people being anxious."

James handed some notes over as a tip. The couriers smiled, thanked him and walked off, eager to get going.

On walking back into the gallery, they found Raphael was sweating. He was in quite a state. Antoinette went over to him, quite concerned.

"Raphael, are you alright? Shall we start to open the wrappings now, to reassure you there is no damage."

"No, no, my sweet, it has just all been too much. I can't stay, I need to go and lie down. We'll unwrap them in the morning. Come on, Constantin, I need to get to the hotel." He almost ran from the gallery. Constantin followed, turned and gave a perplexed look to both of them.

"Oh dear," said James.

"Yes, oh dear. Come on, let's go and sit down. Raphael isn't the only one who's had enough for today."

"You're telling me! What a performance."

"He was genuinely stressed though, James. I'll ring him later to see if he is okay."

With nothing to say to that, he headed up to the little café and ordered hot drinks, even if he could have managed something considerably stronger. Looking out of the window, James noticed some drops of rain. Certainly not a balcony day. 'I really hope this weather isn't set in,' he thought to himself.

Antoinette had followed him into the café and sank into one of the comfortable sofas, which customers loved. The café was quiet, and James was glad that they hadn't witnessed Raphael and his self-pity.

"Thank you, sweetie," said Antoinette as she picked up the coffee that James had bought. She leant against him, then they looked at each other and laughed with relief. "Oh James, I wish the preview was over. I don't think I can stand all this angst."

"You and me both," agreed James. He pulled her to him, and they sat in companionable silence.

* * *

Next morning James was apprehensive. He had spent the previous night at home on his own. His loft apartment generally helped him to rest and relax. Converted from an old warehouse, it was close to St Peter Port, and his penthouse suite afforded wide-ranging views over the harbour and sea. His rooftop terrace was fabulous, but not a place to be in the current dismal weather.

'Just like I feel,' he thought, 'miserable and dismal. Please let Raphael be in a better mood tomorrow.'

* * *

Antoinette had been in her little flat above the gallery. It was in a beautiful spot, looking right out over Fisherman's Wharf and she loved hearing the enjoyable banter as people walked up and down. But she had to admit it was small. Converted at the same time as the gallery itself, and having designed it herself, it was stylish and tasteful, with areas of peaceful pastel painted walls and colourful modern paintings. When the gallery first opened, her little flat seemed ideal. She was so very busy that she wasn't there a great deal. Now she wondered if, perhaps, it was time to find somewhere else. She was never truly away from her gallery responsibilities, and maybe she needed to put more space between work and play. She had wanted to spend time alone, but at the same time she was lonely. Raphael, when she rang, was, of course, fine; just as if nothing at all had been wrong. She poured herself a glass of wine and decided to ring her mother.

"Hello, sweetheart," her Mum enthused, so glad to hear her voice. "How's things?"

"Fine, Mum. Everything is coming together and it won't be long now. But it is stressful – I just want everything to go well."

"But of course, it will. You've worked so hard, there's nothing you haven't done. What can possibly go wrong now? Did Raphael's paintings arrive on time?"

"Yes, they're downstairs now. We're going to look at them all tomorrow."

"There you are then. Please don't worry, Antoinette, or else I'll be worrying too."

"It's just that Raphael is so temperamental, Mum. I know a lot of it is for show, but it can be awkward too because he takes offence so easily."

"He will be on edge, though, won't he? If you're worried, how do you think he feels before such a major exhibition?"

"You're right, Mum, but he's such a successful artist, you wouldn't think he would worry so much."

"Antoinette, a reputation made can also be easily lost. So please don't worry, all is well, and James will make sure everything is OK."

"He will, yes. Thanks Mum, love you so much."

"I love you too, my darling."

After the phone call, Alex was concerned about her daughter. She was normally so much more easy-going. This was such a big thing for her and La Perle, and Alex just wanted everything to go to plan.

Antoinette sipped her wine. 'I care about you Raphael, I really do, but you can make things so hard, especially for James,' she said out loud. 'He is making such an effort to please you; can't you be kinder to him?'

* * *

Next morning, James was the last to arrive, even though he hurried through the damp mist that hung over the sea and Fisherman's Wharf. He had wanted to walk, to get the fresh air, but now wished he had driven. He knew they would be waiting for him.

"Hello!" he shouted as he walked in. Antoinette ran to him, kissed him on the cheek and then led him quickly into the gallery.

"Come on quick, we didn't want to open them until you got here, but Raphael is getting impatient."

"Of course," James said under his breath.

Constantin, standing by the shrink-wrapped paintings, beckoned him over.

"Come, James. Raphael is about to open the first crate."

There was an expectant hush. Then Raphael cracked open the crate to reveal the pictures inside. All four of them simply stood and looked at the open crate.

"Well, here we go," exclaimed Raphael as he lifted out the first picture and stood it against the wall. There was a gasp as James and Antoinette stared at Raphael's masterpiece, the first they had seen. Antoinette didn't quite know what to say. Both she and James had seen many of Raphael's paintings before, but this was nothing like his others. Yes, it was dramatic and abstract, very colourful and flamboyant, much like Raphael himself. As to the quality, she just hoped the others would be better. James, too, just stood and stared.

"You are both very quiet. I can see you are stunned." This was Raphael. "I see you cannot find the right words to describe it."

"Yes, Raphael, that's just it," spluttered James. "I can honestly say I have never seen anything quite like it."

Constantin smothered a smile with his hand.

"Exactly. I did say my paintings were unique."

"Oh, it's certainly unique," agreed James, not knowing whether to laugh or cry.

Antoinette, too, was stunned. "Could we unwrap another, Raphael?" she asked.

"Of course, my dearest, we need to open them all. Constantin, go and get the champagne I brought to celebrate the arrival of my wonderful pieces."

While Raphael was slightly distracted, Antoinette and James looked at each other with something like bewilderment.

"Oh dear," he whispered, "I do hope this one is better."

Something like relief flowed from her when the second one was brought out. This time they could clearly see that the canvas was covered in flowers, in an abstract style, but clear enough to be interpreted as flowers in a field. James thought they looked like poppies, or tulips maybe.

"This one is called 'Remembrance'," Raphael announced. "What do you think, Antoinette?"

"It's really good, Raphael, a wonderful interpretation of the subject. I think people will love it."

"Think? Think? Of course they will love it," he replied crossly. "Really, Antoinette, I expected more enthusiasm from you."

Antoinette smiled hesitantly, feeling embarrassed, and James jumped in to help her.

"Raphael, it's just that we don't quite know what to expect. We've hardly had the chance to take them in yet, but we know your reputation and, yes, they will sell magnificently."

"Yes, well," sniffed Raphael, sulky and offended. "Where is Constantin with that champagne?" He stormed off to find him.

With him out of the room, James and Antoinette breathed a sigh of relief, and whispered to each other.

"Phew, James, if they were all like the first one, I don't know what we'd have done. It's awful. The second is better – I rather like it. Let's hope they get better as we go along."

"I really can't see how he can command the prices he does, though, can you?"

"No, I'm not sure either," agreed Antoinette.

"Oh, Annie, this is so much more stressful than I thought. Let's hope it's worth it."

Raphael returned with the champagne. "Here you are, my darling," he said as he handed her a glass. It was fizzing madly. Raphael still seemed subdued, and the atmosphere was awkward. Then, when all had a glass in hand, Constantin tried to remedy the situation.

"A toast," he said, and lifted his glass. "To Raphael, a magnificent and successful exhibition, and to La Perle, a successful future."

"We'll drink to that," said Antoinette with a laugh.

"Cheers everyone," Constantin continued. "Come on Raphy, it's a nervous time for us all. We have all been so busy. You know James and Antoinette haven't seen your work up close. They need time to assimilate your brilliance. But of course you love it, don't you guys?"

Antoinette was grateful to Constantin. 'Thank you for that' she said to herself.

"Oh, you are so right, Constantin," she said and felt the atmosphere lighten and continue to soften as the other paintings were unwrapped. All were in a similar vein. As Antoinette and James did, indeed, come to more fully understand and appreciate his work, they found it easier to show enthusiasm.

"Now only 'Madrigal' remains," Raphael announced dramatically. He looked at everyone, creating a quiver of excitement. "Do you want to see it now, or shall we retire for a light lunch?"

"No, Raphael, we're dying to see it. Unwrap it, then we can celebrate," Antoinette answered, finding herself excited.

"Right then, here we go," and finally a huge smile appeared as Raphael carefully unwrapped the final painting. "Now, Annie and James, you need to know before you see it that this isn't at all like the others. It isn't framed, it isn't even on a traditional type canvas."

Antoinette glanced quickly and worriedly at James, and an unspoken concern passed between them.

In the meantime, Raphael and Constantin proceeded to unroll a huge piece of canvas and laid it on the floor.

"Remember it's painted on both sides," said Raphael. Then they unwrapped some further material, thin and gauzy. It was silk. "It's more of an art installation than a painting. This silk will be attached to the canvas once it is hung."

"Ah, what a shame we can't yet see it complete, but I can see what you mean about an art installation," enthused James. It was certainly going to be unusual. The painting, as it was, didn't make sense, and probably wouldn't until it was all put together. One fact was certain, though: it was huge. "I think I can understand why it's called Madrigal," he continued.

"You can?" enthused Raphael. "How wonderful; how do you see it?" and for the first time he spoke to James not only in a friendly manner, but also a respectful one.

"Well, to me, Madrigal speaks of the Middle Ages, of music and feasting, tapestries on walls. Then people in clothes made of beautiful rich materials, velvets, veils, sumptuous colours of red, deep blue and dark green. These colours are just like that. Am I right, Raphael?"

"James – my my! You are so perceptive, you have it just right."

James grinned, pleased with himself.

"What do you think, Antoinette?"

"I agree with James; it's so rich and powerful and eye-grabbing. I can't wait to see it in situ."

"Constantin, more champagne all round!" Raphael laughed and positively glowed. "Then we will go for that celebratory lunch."

Before they left, Eleanor arrived. Antoinette noticed how her face positively lit up when she saw Constantin. She's such a lovely young woman, Antoinette told herself, open, friendly, loyal. Constantin is lucky to have her affection.

"Just in time, Eleanor," said Antoinette. "We've just opened all of the paintings and now we're going for lunch. Do you want to come with us? And is there anything I need to know?"

"No, all's fine. And thanks, but I won't join you. I will hold the fort for you and I'd love to look at Raphael's paintings, if you don't mind, Raphael?"

"Of course, you can," he said and smiled warmly at her. "But be careful with them, won't you?"

"I will, don't worry, and thank you."

Just before leaving, Antoinette saw Eleanor sneak up to Constantin.

"I'll see you tonight," she whispered, and blew him a kiss as he left.

Raphael was adamant that the paintings would only go up on Thursday; everyone was relieved as it gave some respite and a calming-down break for all.

* * *

Antoinette's friends, Madeleine and Victoria, were desperate to hear about the exhibition and they persuaded Antoinette that a night out was just what she needed. Antoinette wasn't so sure. There was the big family party on Wednesday night and her nerves were already frayed.

"I'm really not sure I can find the time, and you'll all be at the preview anyway." She sensed their disappointment and relented. "How about a walk? Can you get some time off? The fresh air and exercise will do me good."

They consented immediately, and Antoinette realised she was actually looking forward to seeing them.

"That was a great article in the local paper, wasn't it?" Maddy added, before Antoinette had the chance to end the call.

"What article?" she queried.

"You mean you haven't seen it?"

"Maddy, do you know how busy I've been? And no, I haven't read it. It's strange Mum hasn't told me about it – she reads the paper avidly. I did see the one in the Sunday Times Art Review, but it was only brief."

"Well read it, you'll be really pleased with it."

"I will. Thanks Maddy, I'll go and buy a copy now."

Antoinette had completely forgotten about the article.

Artist Scoop for La Perle
by reporter Daniel West.

Local art gallery La Perle is preparing for a spectacular exhibition as world-renowned artist Raphael Harcourt-Smythe, arrives in Guernsey for an unprecedented display of his unique paintings outside of the world's major cities. The owners are understandably overjoyed.

"We can't understand why he chose our little gallery but, whatever the reason, we are absolutely delighted," enthused joint owner Antoinette Duchenne.

Mr Harcourt-Smythe was unavailable for comment, but his agent, Constantin Patras, sent a report explaining that the artist's motives were entirely altruistic. He wanted to help the Guernsey Lifeboat men who saved his father's life. We understand that an undisclosed sum has already been given, and the profit from the sale one of his paintings is also to be donated.

The exhibition opens next Friday with an invitation-only preview, when celebrities from around the world are expected to attend. Furthermore, Mr Patras told us that the highlight of the exhibition will be the artist's unveiling of his new art installation 'Madrigal'. Details of this masterpiece are being closely guarded.

From Monday, entrance to the exhibition will be free and everyone will be welcome.

* * *

On Wednesday morning, James had other responsibilities. First, he met his sister and family at the airport, drove them to their self-catering cottage, a more sensible idea than a hotel with a very active two-and-a-half-year-old little boy. Luca was, however, adorable and spoilt by his uncle James. Next, he was at the Meribel to catch up with his parents, who had texted to announce their arrival after a very calm crossing. James was eager to see them. He loved Guernsey, but he missed his family. Mum and Dad had wasted no time and were waiting for James in the bar. As he walked in, Julia ran towards him and squeezed him tight.

"Hold on, Mum, I can't breathe!"

"Don't be silly, of course you can. I can't believe we are here with you, it's so lovely to see you. Let me look at you. Mmm... a few dark circles under your eyes. Don't overstretch yourself."

"Mum, this is embarrassing, I'm fine honestly, really fine, but I've been working hard." He looked over his Mum's shoulder to see his Dad, relaxed and comfortable in an armchair, a pint of beer on the table in front of him. James smiled: typical Dad. Johnny beamed as James walked over to him, getting up and shaking hands with his son.

"I'm really glad you could both come and I'm sure you will enjoy your little visit. I can assure you Friday evening will be an event like you will truly never have experienced."

All three sat down and Johnny ordered a drink for James. "What will you have, son?"

"Half of bitter will be fine, Dad, thanks."

"I thought you would have brought Antoinette with you."

"I would have, Mum, but she's gone for a walk with a couple of friends who think they can get some insider gossip about Raphael and the exhibition. They'll be disappointed, though, because she won't tell them anything. Then she's decided to spend the night at her parents to help them arrange for the party tomorrow. Are you OK with the afternoon?"

"Of course! It might have been a bit formal in a restaurant, so I'm glad it's at their house. I'm really looking forward to seeing them again."

"Don't forget, bring your swimsuit, if it's warm enough. You can use their pool."

"That sounds great. Do they need any help, do you think, or contributions for food and drink?"

"No, they were quite happy to arrange it all and see you. It's an exciting time for us all."

"I can't wait!" exclaimed Julia excitably.

"What about you, Dad? You seem quiet."

"No, I'm fine; looking forward to it."

"He's not looking forward to being 'poshed' up in a suit, are you Johnny?"

Johnny smiled indulgently at Julia. "Not quite my style, all these formal events, but I wouldn't miss it for the world."

What could James say? He was embarrassed at what, for Johnny, was a real show of emotion. Changing the subject James said, "What were you reading when I arrived, Dad?"

"Oh, just the local Guernsey paper. Someone just dropped it on the chair over the other side of the room so I thought I'd take a look. Do you want to see it?"

"Wouldn't mind. I'd like to see if there's any more about the gallery. There was a really good report in it last week."

"Will you let us see it, sweetheart?" asked Julia.

"Of course." James picked up the paper. He was perplexed when he saw one of the articles on an inside page.

Huge Disappointment for the Guernsey Lifeboat
Reporter Daniel West

Skipper of the St Peter Port lifeboat, Simon Batiste, is overwhelmed with disappointment after a generous donation by world-famous artist Mr Raphael Harcourt-Smythe could not be cashed when presented at the bank. Mr Harcourt-Smythe, who has exhibited at the Tate Gallery in London, was horrified and acutely embarrassed and apologetic when contacted by reporters at his London studio.

"You cannot imagine how distraught and embarrassed I am, but you see I have many different bank accounts and never really know what is in each one. I will, of course, present the Lifeboat fund with another cheque when I am in Guernsey for my exhibition" Mr Batiste was heartened at this news but said if reporters hadn't tracked him down, he wasn't sure that Mr Harcourt-Smythe would have contacted the skipper and, as yet, they still hadn't heard from him.

James was quiet.

"Are you alright, sweetheart?" said Julia.

"Of course, I just have a lot on my mind. Anyway, how's the hotel? It comes highly recommended."

"Oh, it's lovely, and we decided to upgrade to a sea view, deluxe room. We have a fabulous view over the harbour and marina."

James found it hard to concentrate. He couldn't figure out what was happening.

'Should I tell Annie?' he asked himself, but what would be the point? She had enough on her mind. No, he decided, he would keep it to himself and ponder it alone. He only hoped it would have no ramifications for the exhibition, but then really, how could it?

"Are you sure you're alright?" his mother stressed.

"Yes, no problem, but if you don't mind, I think I'll go home now you're settled in. I have an early morning tomorrow for the hanging."

"The hanging?" Julia exclaimed.

"The picture hangings, Mum, at the gallery. They go up tomorrow, so that it leaves us Friday to arrange everything else around the paintings. Raphael would go mad if even one looked to be overshadowed, even by a plant leaf. He is frantically particular."

"Oh, I see," said Julia, laughing. "You go on home then. I think Georgia is coming over later while Oliver looks after Luca. See you tomorrow at Alex and Charles' place." She gave him a peck on the cheek. Johnny waved as he watched his son leave.

* * *

Next morning, James arrived at almost the same time as Antoinette was unlocking the gallery door. He strolled down the wharf.

"Everything OK, James?"

"Yes, fine," James answered, as Annie turned off the alarm, and he followed her in.

"I can't wait to see the paintings in situ, especially Madrigal."

"I know. How long do you think it will take to hang them all?" James asked.

"Hopefully not too long if we all muck in to help. But Raphael may not want us to even touch them, let alone risk hanging one up."

"You're right there, Annie." They both stood stock still, their mouths agape.

"What the…?" but no words came out of Antoinette's mouth.

James continued for her: "You mean, how come all the paintings are already hung?"

Both were mesmerised and they slowly walked around and looked at all the exhibits.

"Wow, James, it looks fantastic." She was in genuine awe. "Raphael and Constantin must have come here last night; they must have wanted to do it alone."

"It must have taken them hours, but it looks absolutely stunning," agreed James.

"Let's have a look at Madrigal." They had only seen it on the ground and now, seeing it displayed fully, it was huge. "I can't believe it, James. It is absolutely nothing like any of his other work. What do you think?"

"I think that it is really something! Nothing like how I imagined it would be."

As explained by Raphael, the canvas was painted on both sides. The colours were rich and vibrant, but not garish. They could see there was real pattern to it, yet everything blended together and their eyes flicked continuously over the colours; red, ochre, lapis, green with splashes of gold, and what, in the Middle Ages, would have been called 'cloth of gold'. Then, there was the silk covering, hazy and almost transparent, but reflecting the colours beautifully. Nor was the silk just laid on the canvas like plastic wrapping. Rather, it was layered and ruched in a complex way, giving substance but yet never hiding the myriad rich colours beneath. In fact, its virtual luminescence made the fabric almost glow and shimmer. They both stood for many moments, silently admiring Madrigal, and then the rest.

"Has it all been worth it, then?" James asked. "The worry, stress, finding the money to finance it, and – last but not least – putting up with Raphael, his moods, sulks and very aggravating habits?"

"He isn't that bad; I see a different side of him to you."

"Well, I wish I could."

Antoinette thumped him lightly on the arm and laughed. "Stop it, James. The answer to your question must surely be yes, yes, yes! Come on, let's go and get a coffee, I certainly need something." She took James' hand and they walked together out of the gallery, heading for a little café with chairs outside, just further down the wharf. Both were relaxed, optimistic and supremely happy.

"Oh no! I recognise that voice," said Antoinette and sure enough, Raphael and Constantin turned the corner onto the wharf and were obviously heading for the gallery.

"I don't know why you think we should come back now. We've been up nearly all night and I need to go back and sleep," moaned Raphael.

"You can soon, but surely you can see we need to come and explain about the paintings."

"I suppose you're right." Raphael spotted Antoinette at the café. "Here you are, my darling. We were just coming to see you." Then he bent down and gave her a long kiss.

"We wanted to explain why we did them ourselves last night," Constantin said.

"Thank you," answered Antoinette, "but it's fine. We've worked out why you wanted to get on and do it yourselves. We can understand, can't we James? There's no need to go to the gallery. You can go back to the hotel and sleep, Raphael, knowing how fantastic it looks, and the star of the show, Madrigal, is magnificent – we both love it."

"Well of course you do, how could you not, my sweetheart, my dearest darling."

James moaned to himself, 'here we go again!'

"Right Constantin. Come on, let's go. I'm so tired and I have had no breakfast." Raphael dragged him away, back down the wharf to the hotel. Constantin looked back, smiled and waved at them with a distinct look of amusement in his dark, soulful eyes.

"Do you want to go and rest too, Annie?"

"Actually, I think I will. I'm very tired. I've got so much on my mind, and I didn't sleep too well last night."

"Nor me. I really do think I will be glad when Friday night is all over."

"You and me both."

"Go on then, back home and get some rest. We need to be at your parents' this afternoon."

"Oh, I know, it's all too hectic." She laid her head on his shoulder.

"Come on then."

She got up and made her way back to her little flat. She waved to James as he started walking, probably back to his flat; he needed to rest too.

"See you this afternoon," he called. "It will be lovely; we can all relax."

"See you later, James."

In her flat, after taking off her shoes, she just lay on the bed and almost immediately fell into a deep sleep.

James was not so lucky. However hard he tried, he only managed to doze, then gave up, deciding to get ready for the family party. 'I'm so glad my family is here to celebrate with us,' he said to himself.

Chapter Nine

The Duchennes were a true Guernsey family, going back generations and with a heritage that meant they were well-known on the island. In America, they would be called 'old money'. Like many, their relatives had suffered through the German Occupation. Despite the passage of time, it had proved impossible to rid the island of its memories; the firmly built remnants of the Germans were still apparent across the islands. After the war, the family had recovered well and their businesses had prospered. Like many islanders, Alex and Charles owned a yacht and enjoyed visiting neighbouring islands, and often sailed over to France for the weekend. They already had an enviable lifestyle but were looking forward to Gabriel taking over more responsibility, freeing up their time to relax and further enjoy their life. They were especially pleased that both of their children had decided to stay on the island. So many had to leave to find work, and house prices could be prohibitive.

Alex and Charles knew they had a privileged life. Both were healthy, if perhaps a little weather-beaten from yachting, Alex's hair had been lightened by the sun and sea breezes, while Charles seemed to be getting greyer by the day. They were looking forward to seeing Julia and Johnny. Despite different backgrounds, they had become good friends since Antoinette and James had opened La Perle. Like Antoinette and Gabriel, Alex and Charles were tall, but neither so slim as they used to be, and this bothered them not at all. Charles was looking forward to a fishing trip with Johnny, taking their yacht 'Guernsey Gannet' out to where he knew shoals of mackerel were currently running nearby.

The party was everything both families had hoped it would be. Alex knew that having an informal get-together was better than being in a formal restaurant. Luckily, the weather was fine, so everyone was able to stay outside for most of the afternoon.

"Where have you been?" asked Alex as Antoinette arrived late.

"Oh, don't moan at me, Mum. I was shattered and fell asleep; then had to get ready in a rush. I'm here now though."

"Course you are. I'm sorry, I know how tired you must be. Come and meet Georgia and Oliver – they've brought their son Luca, and he is absolutely delightful."

Antoinette did, indeed, feel drained and sluggish but knew that the afternoon would be pleasant and she tried to relax. James, however, looked almost radiant, sparkling even. His straw-coloured hair always lightened in the sun, highlighting the reddish hints which were also there. She knew he was delighted that his family were here. It was easy to forget that he didn't see them often, unlike herself, whose family was on the doorstep so they could see each other almost daily. She was glad everyone was enjoying themselves eating, drinking and laughing; she took a glass of wine and mingled, glad to have something not connected to the gallery.

Charles and Johnny were happily chatting together.

"Do you fancy a spot of fishing Johnny, while you are over? Will you have time, do you think?"

"That would be great. What are we likely to catch?"

"Mostly mackerel probably. They often come inshore in shoals, so we'll definitely catch something."

"Can't think when I last went sea fishing, Charles. I'll look forward to it."

"Excellent. I'll take us out on the yacht. You used to do some salmon fishing, didn't you?"

"Oh yes, still do. The fishing club has a stretch of the river Tweed. Costs the earth, of course, but there's nowhere quite like the Tweed. It's a fair way to go though, so I don't get there as often as I'd like," answered Johnny, disappointment clear in his voice.

"Mackerel fishing's a bit different, Johnny."

"Oh, but it will be an enjoyable change. I'm really looking forward to it. Where do you moor your yacht then, Charles?"

"St Peter Port Marina. Had a mooring there for years. Go and search her out when you go for a look around the marina. You can't miss her – the 'Guernsey Gannet'. She has a beautiful paining of a gannet on the side.

"I will. The Meribel is almost across from the marina, so it's just right for a little stroll. But look, you've provided all this today, I can't let you pay for the fishing trip as well."

"You can, and you will! It's not often we see you so don't argue."

"That's very generous, Charles. Thank you," replied Johnny appreciatively.

* * *

Julia, too, was relishing the opportunity to mix and catch up on any news.

"You look wonderful," she said to Laura, Gabriel's wife.

"I'm anything but, Julia, I'm almost baby elephant size!"

"No, really, you are positively glowing. When is the baby due?"

"Any time now, and it can't be soon enough," laughed Laura.

"Alex must be so excited, it being her first grandchild; I know we were when Luca came along."

"She's a wonderful mother-in-law, and not everyone can say that, can they?"

"No, and I certainly hope Oliver says the same as you."

"Are you looking forward to the exhibition?" asked Laura.

"We wouldn't have missed coming for anything. I'm so proud of them both, they've worked so hard to make a success of La Perle."

"Do you know any of the famous people who are supposedly coming?"

"I don't, but I'm looking forward to seeing who is there."

"Yes, me too."

Antoinette looked over to see James smiling as he walked over to speak to his father. She followed him and he turned and smiled at her also.

"You look happy, James," she said, looking into his emerald eyes, sparkling like a sometimes Guernsey sea.

"What's not to be happy about? Surrounded by my family and with a major exhibition in hand and my beautiful partner by my side," he said. Antoinette, however, looked hesitant and he noticed her face cloud over. "Don't worry, Annie, everything will be fine. We have worked too hard for it not to be."

"You're right, and as you say, all our families will be there to support us. I think I'm going to leave now; I need a restful evening. Tomorrow is 'the' day, you know."

"How could I forget? Go on; you go. I'll hold out here for a little while longer and see you at the gallery in the morning."

"Make it early," Antoinette emphasised.

"Yes ma'am," he said, saluting her. She laughed, knowing that James would really help her get through it all. She walked over to say her farewells, and James shouted back to her. "Antoinette, please try to relax. Tomorrow is a day to enjoy the fruits of our labours, to remember the day joyfully as a special time."

In the end no-one had bothered to take a swim. Somehow everyone was happy to just enjoy each other's company and conversation, wine, good food and great company flowed throughout. Julia sought out Alex.

"Thank you so much, Alex, for making this such an effort today. It's been wonderful. I've really enjoyed it and it has set the scene for tomorrow, hasn't it?"

"It certainly has, it isn't every day we get to go to such a high-profile event. Did you hear that the exhibition had a small write up in The Times?"

"I know, that's great isn't it? Quite famous, our two children, something to be proud of. Now I must find my husband and then we're off,." She and Alex had a friendly hug. "Johnny, where are you?..."

* * *

Suddenly it was Friday morning. Antoinette was full of energy; she had slept far better than she expected, felt refreshed and keen to get going. Down in the gallery, it wasn't long before James joined her, and Eleanor wasn't far behind. The day flew by and it seemed as if the world and his wife had a reason to call. With all the caterers, the wine merchants, the florist, the cleaners, it was indeed hectic, but by late afternoon all seemed ready. The string quartet had rung and said they would arrive at 6.30pm. There was literally nothing more to do, and all three walked around together. Antoinette admired all the flowers. She loved flowers and had thought she might do the arrangements herself but common-sense took over and when she looked at the end result, she knew it had been for the best. Hanging from the gallery between the exhibits were festoons of greenery interlaced with flowers, reflecting the rich colours of Madrigal. On the tables were bowls of flowers in natural styles and, in the entrance, toilets and the seating areas were scented lilies, hedgerow flowers and some early autumn-coloured leaves. All enhanced the paintings and especially Madrigal, which was certainly the star of the show; large, majestic but also delicate and almost ephemeral, the silk and fine tulle rustling, as any small breeze fluttered the material.

All three knew that the gallery looked magnificent and there was nothing they could do to improve it. The weather, too, looked set to complement, with a blue sky, a slight breeze, and the promise of a warm clear night. Collapsing into chairs and drinking much-needed refreshment, they were exhausted but elated.

"Is the champagne on chill, Eleanor?"

"Yes, Annie, don't worry."

"Are the chairs for the quartet in the right place, do you think?"

"Exactly as we planned, Annie. Don't worry."

"Are we sure 8pm is the right time to serve the buffet?"

"Definitely," answered James, "and before you ask, yes, there is masses of food and drink." James looked at Eleanor who smiled and rolled her eyes, yet she understood all this last-minute panic. "Antoinette, just go and rest and then you need to get ready. Our families and friends are coming at 6.30, remember?"

"Oh yes, I'd forgotten. It was a good idea of your letting them come early – it makes them seem special, which they are of course."

"Annie…"

"Yes, OK, I'm going, and Eleanor too. So go on, you go home, and we'll see you at 6.30. What about you, James?"

"I've brought my clothes here; I'm not going home. I'll have a bit of fresh air and then change here."

"You can change in my flat and have a shower."

"Sure, Annie?"

"Of course I'm sure, you idiot. I can't have you changing in the gents!" With that, she headed to the stairs and her little flat, leaving James alone with his thoughts.

* * *

When James came out from the shower, he found Antoinette dressed and ready to go.

"Antoinette, you look so beautiful." She was dressed in a long white shift dress which emphasised her tall, slim body. Her hair was swept up, but casually, so that strands of hair fell softly around her face and shoulders. The dress was enhanced by painterly swirls in purple and silver, reflecting and highlighting her violet eyes. Earrings of dark amethyst draped down almost to her shoulders, around which was a silk pashmina of the finest, flimsy quality and in the palest lilac.

"Actually, I have a present for you," he told her, and out of his jacket pocket he gave her a small box. "There you are, Miss Aquarius, I know how much you love your amethysts." When she opened it, she found an exquisite amethyst bracelet, which she put on immediately.

"Oh, thank you, James. It's absolutely perfect and completes the outfit."

"It does. Now I need to get ready too."

"I'll leave you to it," she answered, and went out to the gallery.

It didn't take him long and he was able to join Antoinette well before any of the guests were expected. There was a definite air of expectation, Antoinette busying herself once again, checking that all was as it should be. She turned when James entered and felt a fluttering in her stomach. He looked so handsome, she said to herself, and so kind and thoughtful.

"Well, you look pretty good yourself," she said to him, trying hard to suppress the feelings she currently had for him. His bespoke suit was grey, with a grey shirt of a darker shade, and a dark green silk tie which highlighted those deep, rich, emerald eyes. The sun of the last months had given him a deep tan and he looked healthy and fit.

"Not long now. I actually wish they would start to arrive, even if it is early."

"No-one likes to arrive too early at this kind of event, James, do they?"

"No, you're right," James was just saying, when the door opened and the first guests emerged, who were actually reporters and photographers. The TV cameras had confirmed they would come too, but at a given time of 8pm.

"So, this is it," James told himself, and no-one needed to have worried. The families felt privileged to be given a first look and also to be there when any important guests arrived, and all were impressed with the food and champagne, which flowed freely. There was lobster, crab, scallops, a griddle in a corner for anyone who wanted a hot steak. There was even caviar and further down the scale were bacon rolls, hand-cut chips, pasta, homemade bread and specially prepared courses for alternative tastes and needs. Puddings were no less generous, hot and cold, lashings of cream cheese, figs and grapes. It was a veritable feast and beautifully laid out and adorned with fresh flowers, candles and bowls of rose petals scattered around. There were a lot of people in a small space so that they spread out along the upper mezzanine, some even moving outside to take in the harbour and sea air.

Julia just couldn't believe how excited she was. She had been to exhibitions at La Perle before but none had such an atmosphere. There were so many people to watch, delicious food and her pride in her son. She recognised famous faces, hardly believing they had made the effort to come to the exhibition. But then it was obviously a place to be. 'And I'm here too,' she said to herself and she felt privileged. Julia stood mesmerised, seeing all the dazzling outfits and confident smiles. Also, there was money here tonight and she knew that was good.

"Mum", James said, as he took Julia unawares. "Are you enjoying yourself?"

"Oh, sweetheart, it's wonderful. All these people and so many famous faces. Isn't that the famous model over there, looking at Madrigal?"

"I rather think it is," James replied proudly. "I'll introduce you if you like, she's really very nice."

"Would you? Oh, how exciting!" and she walked off with James, eager to be introduced. She would probably never have another chance to mingle with the 'in' crowd.

Luca, a bubbly child, was mesmerised and eager to explore. He had James' blond hair and was adorable. Sticky fingers needed to be watched out for, but Georgia assiduously followed him around. Then more people piled in, seemingly all at once, excited and oohing and aahing, not just at the paintings but at everything, and the whole atmosphere was buzzing. But, as 7.45pm approached, one person was missing.

"Where is Raphael?" Antoinette asked James agitatedly. "Everyone wanted to meet him but he isn't here! What is he thinking?…"

"I know what he's thinking Annie, and you should know too. He'll be waiting until everyone has arrived, and are waiting expectantly, so that he can then make a grand entrance," replied an exasperated James.

"Honestly James. Surely, he isn't so vain and arrogant?"

Then, just as James had predicted, Raphael appeared. The room fell suddenly silent, as everyone turned to look at him. He had dispensed with his bohemian apparel and, instead, was wearing a dinner suit, complete with deep blue bow tie and black patent leather shoes. He had a captive audience.

James, however, was not impressed. "Typical," he muttered under his breath. "He had to outdo everyone and make a grand entrance!" But, at the same time, he felt quite relaxed, and could laugh at Raphael; he knew him well by now.

Raphael stood on the steps and shouted "Welcome, welcome everyone! I am delighted to greet you all, as, no doubt, you are delighted to be here and to meet me. I can't imagine there is anyone here who doesn't know me; my fame goes before me, of course. I am Raphael Harcourt-Smythe. I don't need to thank you all for coming as I'm sure you know it is a great privilege for you to be here. However, I recommend you make haste to snap up my paintings. Everyone I know will want to buy, so I urge you to purchase now, before we celebrate with this wonderful food and drink."

James watched Antoinette escort the reporters and TV crew up to the gallery office. She told Raphael where they were, and he glided across the room looking full of himself. On his way up to the office, he shouted "Excuse me, my friends, but the media has arrived, so I must leave you for now. They are desperate to speak to me, you see, and take my photograph, of course. I will look so good in the newspapers!" No-one seemed to take much notice, however, as he disappeared into the office to meet the press. Quite what they thought of their interviewee wasn't clear, but James asked them to take some shots of the event so that La Perle would get some publicity too. They seemed happy with that, but they soon left, despite being invited to join the buffet. They rejoined their guests as everyone made their way up to the mezzanine and the fabulous buffet. "Oh, I forgot to mention to you my special guests," Raphael began again, "Remember I will be donating the profit from one of my sales to the Guernsey Lifeboat. You see, I am not just a great artist, but a generous one too." Everyone clapped and murmured to one another.

'Thank goodness I won't have to put up with him any longer,' James said to himself. 'What he never said, though, was why he had already given them a cheque which had bounced. I still don't know what is going on with him.'

After his speech and photographs with the media, Raphael sought out Antoinette.

"My darling, you look delectable," he said and held her in an embrace. "Shall we stroll around the gallery while everyone else is checking out the food?"

"So, what do you think, Raphael? It's a massive turnout. I don't think we could have fitted in many more."

"Perfect, my Antoinette, perfect, but then I told you it would be."

"You did."

Raphael took her hand and kissed it. "Now, have we sold any yet?"

"I think just one so far," she said, leading him to a painting with a red dot. "More will go after all the eating and drinking."

"It will – that's how it always seems to be. No, come on, let's go and eat and drink ourselves, before all the champagne disappears."

James was keeping watch. His Mum had brought him a plate of food and a glass of champagne and he sat down to enjoy it, along with the string quartet, which was playing at a perfect pitch, making sure they didn't overwhelm the atmosphere so that people could converse easily.

"Your music is lovely," he told the musicians, "absolutely perfect for the occasion. Have you played at previews like this before?"

"A couple of times," the double bass player replied, "but mostly we play at weddings. We do concerts as well, of course, but these events really do help boost our income."

"I'm sure they do, but why don't you have a rest and help yourself to some refreshments."

"Thank you, that's kind. I'm sure we can all do with a drink."

James was very satisfied: it just couldn't have gone any better.

Upstairs, Eleanor had been looking for Antoinette.

"What's wrong, Eleanor?" She seemed quite distraught.

"Have you seen Constantin?" she said urgently.

"No, what's the problem?"

"I can't find him!" There was almost panic in her voice.

"Don't get upset, he's probably just nipped out to get some fresh air, or on an errand for Raphael."

"No, you don't understand. He hasn't turned up tonight at all. He just isn't here."

"Don't be silly; he must be, surely. Did he not come in after Raphael arrived?"

"No, that's just it, he didn't, and of course he promised to be here, he had to be here, he wouldn't just not come."

Then, on thinking what Eleanor had said, she couldn't recall having seen him either. She had assumed he was there; he always was. Certainly, this was strange. She tried to calm Eleanor, and promised to ask Raphael where Constantin was.

Meantime, in his watching phase, James noticed that some more red dots had appeared on the paintings and he wondered who had dealt with the sale. Moreover, James couldn't believe his eyes when he saw there was a large red dot on Madrigal. He was stunned and immediately went in search of Antoinette.

Antoinette was glad she had bought Eleanor a dress for the opening. It hadn't been over-expensive, but it was a designer dress, floor length and off the shoulder, in a soft teal colour. She looked great. Simply the fact that she now felt on an equal level with guests, she was confident, animated, a real asset to the gallery. She was so enjoying herself, she almost floated around, socialising, helping, so much a part of everything. Antoinette knew she would miss her when she went back to university. Yet, Antoinette was sad to see she was no longer enjoying herself. The sparkle had gone, she was truly worried about Constantin. Of course, she realised the relationship had developed over the past month, but it seemed more serious than she had thought. She didn't want Eleanor to worry, but then, she already was. It was more than strange that Constantin hadn't appeared – but why? Where was he?'

"There you are, James! I've been looking for you. Listen, have you seen Constantin? Eleanor is worried that he hasn't made an appearance tonight and Raphael hasn't said anything."

"Never mind that now, Annie," he answered rather abruptly. "Have you noticed that Madrigal has sold?" Antoinette's eyes opened wide, both with surprise and pleasure.

"No, I didn't know. Come on, show me!" and they both dashed up to see; plus James needed to see that he hadn't imagined it.

"Oh, my God, James, I can't believe it. We need to tell Raphael...where is he?"

"He was up in the mezzanine." Then, before Annie and James could get his attention, Raphael went towards the edge of the mezzanine and looked down at the lower exhibition area. With a glass of champagne in his hand, he called for everyone's attention. He was about to make another speech.

"My dearest friends, I want to thank you all for being here today and I would like us all to raise a glass and toast this very successful exhibition. I know you all love my work, and I am delighted to tell you that my masterpiece, Madrigal, has been sold." There were gasps, people hardly believing such an extravagant exhibit could sell so quickly. "Now, I know you may want to know who was so eager to buy it, and how disappointed you are knowing you now can't now purchase it yourselves, but the buyer wishes to remain anonymous, and has bought it at an undisclosed sum, but you all know it will have commanded a huge price." Raphael swayed slightly.

"He's drunk," Antoinette murmured. "James, tell him not to say any more."

Just then, as Raphael was about to continue, there was a wail and a cry. It was Luca, who was obviously tired and fractious, and ready to go home. Antoinette made her way towards Georgia to offer her flat so that Luca could sleep, but she never made it. Raphael's voice boomed throughout the gallery.

"Is that a child?" he shouted and pointed to Luca. "What is a child doing at this, my exhibition? No-one asked my permission for a child to attend! Just imagine the danger of a child damaging the paintings. Well, I can't believe it – take him out at once."

James was incensed and shouted back, "Raphael, he's my nephew and he has been as good as gold." Georgia was mortified as everyone stared at her. Antoinette quickly went to her, seeing how upset and embarrassed she was. Antoinette moved Georgia and Luca out of Raphael's sight, and up to her flat.

Raphael was almost red with rage.

He's going into meltdown, James realised. He had to get him to stop this rant; what was he thinking? James approached him as Raphael started to sway again.

"Come on – stop this, Raphael, you can't behave like this." Before Raphael had the chance to argue, James dragged him away into a quiet corner.

"What are you doing? Get off me, how dare you, James?"

"Look, you're drunk. Can't you see that you have upset everyone, not to mention my lovely sister? People are starting to leave; the evening is ruined, you've spoiled everything. I've never liked you and I really think I was right not to."

"Don't speak to me like that." Raphael was belligerent but seemed to have sobered up a little. "Let them go anyway, I've sold Madrigal and that's what I came to do. Now, if you'll excuse me, I think I shall leave now and go back to my hotel and celebrate. Yes, celebrate; it's been a great success as far as I can see."

"Go then, I don't care." James was furious. "And also, where is Constantin? He hasn't been here all evening."

"What does it matter to you where he is; he works for me and I tell him what to do. Goodnight!" He loudly shouted 'goodnight' to those who were left. Raphael then disappeared out into the night and at that point James didn't care where he went.

"What a sorry end to a wonderful event," James said to his mother who, totally confused, was sitting with Johnny wondering what to do. The string quartet was also unsure and had stopped playing. "Don't worry, don't play anymore, just go. I'll settle your fee another day." They didn't need any persuading and hurriedly put their instruments away and headed out the door.

Antoinette had missed most of the action and when she came back into the gallery, everything had quietened down. Visitors quietly retrieved their coats and wraps, embarrassingly shaking James' hand as they left. What could they say?

Antoinette had left Georgia, Oliver and Luca to stay in her flat for a while, letting Luca sleep before going back to their cottage.

"What the hell has happened here, James? We will never live this down."

"Yes we will. None of this is our fault, people will know that."

"I hope you're right; I really do."

"In the meantime, Annie, we still need to work with Raphael. We have a contract and he needs to fulfil it."

"Oh, James, I'm so sorry. You were right about Raphael."

"I'm not proud of being right and, to be honest, people will just see his outburst as nothing but an artist's temperament. In a funny sort of way, the attention may even do his reputation some good, rather than the other way round."

"You know, you may well be right there."

"Come on, let's see the rest of our families off, assure them that all is well and that we are fine. Madrigal is still sold and we will get our 20%, we'll make sure of that."

"Where do you think Constantin is, James? Eleanor is really worried about him. She said he was so looking forward to him being here. What could have happened to him?"

"Let's wait until tomorrow. I'm sure there is a very simple answer."

"I hope so. Where's Eleanor, by the way?"

"I told her to go home and not worry, but I know she will."

"Thank you, James. I honestly don't know what I'd do without you in my life."

James took her in his arms. "You don't need to thank me, you know that." She looked up at him and suddenly she kissed him, at first gently on the lips and then more passionately.

"I love you, Antoinette. I've loved you for so long; I would do anything for you."

Antoinette's eyes misted over. "And I love you too, James," and then realised what she had said. She didn't regret her words; she had suddenly realised that she really did love him. 'How could I not have realised this before?' she asked herself.

"What did you say?" questioned James in disbelief.

"I said, I love you too!" And she meant it.

James could hardly believe it! Suddenly, a catastrophic ending to the exhibition had turned into the best day of his life. His family, waiting quietly to leave, had noticed all, and Julia smiled to herself contentedly.

Walking towards their families, Antoinette said to her parents, "Would it be alright to stay with you tonight? Let Luca have some sleep?" They all walked out onto a balmy, starry night, a pale moon shining on the sea.

* * *

It was a bleary-eyed Antoinette who turned up at the gallery on a late Saturday morning. She had arranged for the caterers to arrive at about 11.30 to clear up from the night before. Now, she wished she had left it until Sunday. 'Anyway, I'm here now,' she told herself. She switched off the alarm, relieved that Georgia had managed to set it when they left. Luca had settled down and when they left to go back to their self-catering cottage, all was calm. Annie had no spring in her step; she knew everything would be a mess, but it had been worth it, hadn't it? Madrigal and other paintings had been sold. Please, just don't let Raphael's behaviour affect the gallery's reputation. And James, what happened there? It was all so strange. Somehow, Raphael had helped clear her mind; she now saw him in a different way and knew she had been blinded by him and felt quite embarrassed about it. Yet it brought out, too, the realisation that it was James who she loved. 'How could I not have seen it before? I have been stupid,' she thought. 'I could have lost him.' And that sent shivers down her spine. Yes, she was jaded and tired but she accepted, too, that the elation she felt deep inside was the real thing. She was now sure that she really loved James, and, if for no other reason, the exhibition had been worth it.

Chapter Ten

The gallery certainly looked like the morning after the night before. Still, there had been no damage and Antoinette mulled over the exhibition, exhilarated that all gone well, except for Raphael's outburst. Such a stupid, arrogant man. She went straight to the office and made some coffee. Fortunately, the gallery and café were closed for the day, so there was no rush. Sipping her hot coffee, she went back downstairs, eager to stroll around and refresh her memory of what had sold. Somehow, something seemed wrong, yet initially, she was unsure what. Then she realised, and let out a scream, fainting, falling to the floor, spilling coffee. Coming round, she remembered, but her mind was muzzy. "Madrigal!" she shouted, "Madrigal! Where is Madrigal?"

Madrigal was nowhere to be seen. There was a huge gap where it had hung, a vacant space where it had draped down from the ceiling into the gallery. Finally, she realised. "Madrigal is gone, it must have been stolen. Oh, God, what has happened here?" she called out. Again she felt dizzy and faint, but managed to sit on the stairs to stop herself collapsing to the floor. Managing to find her phone in her pocket, she rang James.

"James!" she cried. "Please come."

"Antoinette, where are you? What's wrong?"

"I'm at the gallery, James. Please come now. It's gone!"

"What's gone, Antoinette, tell me." But Antoinette just started to sob.

"Just come, please. Now, James, now."

In a panic, James set off immediately for the gallery. He couldn't imagine what was wrong. All kinds of scenarios flashed through his mind; she had been attacked, she was seriously ill, injured, or perhaps had a bad fall. Her call just hadn't made any sense, but he knew for certain that something was very wrong. He was grateful that Guernsey was a small island, and he would be at the gallery in minutes. When he walked in, she was sitting on the gallery steps, bewildered and clearly very shocked and confused. She held out her arms to him, and he held her in an enveloping embrace.

"Annie, darling, what is it?"

"The painting, M... M... Madrigal," she stuttered, "it's gone, James. It's gone."

"What do you mean, gone?" and he, too, was confused.

"Look! Just look where it should be... it's not there, not there."

Then he turned and saw that where the huge canvas should have been there was an empty space.

"My God, Madrigal!" He too looked around, thinking it would be somewhere else. But no. He sat down on the steps beside Antoinette, his mind somewhat blank. Then he understood. "It's been stolen, Annie, stolen. What do we do?"

"I don't know, I don't know."

James sat, his head in his hands, Antoinette staring blankly ahead, both totally shocked.

"How could this have happened?" James whispered. "We haven't imagined it, have we? It is real?"

"Yes, it's real, very real," Antoinette whispered back.

Then James was energised. "We need to call the police. I'm going to do that now. You stay here, don't move."

Still stunned, Antoinette had no plan to move, but felt relieved that something was happening.

Chapter Eleven

"Police! Emergency!" he shouted when someone came on the line. "How can I help you?"

"Please send the police now, now. A theft, an awful theft."

"Calm down, sir, calm down, and tell me properly. Did you say you've had a break in? Where are you, sir?"

"At the gallery."

"Which gallery would that be, sir?"

"La Perle, La Perle art gallery."

"Okay sir, and what has been stolen?"

"A painting. Look, you need to send someone, now! It's a catastrophe!"

"Just a painting sir?" the person at the other end of the line now wondering what kind of over-panicked person she was speaking to.

"No, no, not just a painting," James emphasised, starting to feel frustrated.

"What else then sir?"

"No, I mean it's a special painting! It's worth ten million pounds!"

"Really, sir?", she replied, trying to keep the disbelief out of her voice.

"Yes, really." He wanted to shout, but tried to calm down, hoping he was being believed. "Please send someone."

"Okay, someone will be with you as soon as possible. Has anyone been hurt, sir?"

"No, no-one, but it's still very serious."

"Yes, I can see how upset you are. So can you tell me please, who you are and where you are?"

"My name is James Kerrissey and my gallery partner is Antoinette Duchenne. We are at La Perle gallery, it's on the old Fisherman's Wharf."

"Someone will be with you shortly, sir."

"Thank you." James collapsed back onto the stairs. There was nothing to do now but wait. James wished someone could take responsibility and tell them what they ought to do. Neither of them moved, and neither spoke, realising that Madrigal really had been stolen.

It didn't seem long before they heard voices at the door; it was the police, a man and a woman. They entered without knocking, and she was the first to speak.

"Mr James Kerrissey?" she asked, and he confirmed who he was. "Are you the person who called the police?"

"Yes, it was me."

"Okay, I can see you are both very shocked, but these stairs aren't the most suitable place for us to question you. Is there, perhaps, somewhere a bit more comfortable and private? Then you can tell us about it."

"We can go to the office, just at the top of these stairs," James volunteered. He got up and then pulled Antoinette to her feet. The office was certainly more comfortable with sofas and low coffee tables.

"This is very nice, much more congenial," said the police officer. She introduced herself. "I'm Detective Sergeant Fontaine, and this is Detective Constable Swann," she said as she pointed to the officer who sat beside her. "Dean," she said, addressing her constable, "I wonder if you could rustle up some drinks for us all." The sergeant realised the gallery owners needed reviving if she was to get an accurate story from them. The constable wandered over to a corner where he had spotted a kettle. "Now, can you introduce yourselves properly?" Sergeant Fontaine began. They both explained that they were the joint owners of the gallery. "So, can you tell us what has happened?"

Antoinette looked distressed, but James tried to explain. He told her how the exhibition had been planned for months, right up to the previous evening and the opening night.

"And when did you notice that a painting was missing?"

"It was me," Antoinette replied softly. "When I arrived here this morning, I switched off the alarm then strolled around the gallery. The exhibition isn't open today, but I'd come to let the caterers and cleaners in. I noticed that Madrigal wasn't anywhere in the gallery. I couldn't believe it and looked around to see if it had been moved. Silly really, but I was so confused. Then I rang James who came straight away."

"So neither of you live here in the gallery?"

"I do, I have a small flat upstairs, but I didn't stay here last night, I stayed over at my parents' in Fort George."

"And I live in St Peter Port," added James, "I work there too. I only help out here when necessary."

"Okay, so one painting is missing, which happened to be the star exhibit. You are both totally shocked, so it must have been valuable."

"Oh yes, it certainly was valuable, insured for ten million pounds!" explained James.

Meanwhile, DC Swann had brought over some hot drinks, and they were welcome.

"How much?" the sergeant asked, aghast at what James had told her.

"You heard right," confirmed Antoinette. "You see, it was a very special exhibit. The artist, Raphael Harcourt-Smythe, is a world-renowned artist. His paintings always command high prices and we believed ourselves privileged to hold one of his exhibitions here."

"Okay, so do either of you have any idea who stole the painting, or where it might be now?"

"No!" exclaimed Antoinette, "I just can't imagine who could have done it. It makes no sense."

"What's more," continued James, "the painting had been sold last night to an anonymous buyer for an undisclosed sum. Raphael was playing things close to his chest, but he would have had to tell us eventually as we would deal with the sale and take our commission."

"Yet, someone who knew your alarm system, and the value of the painting, did steal it. There can't be many people who knew both, so you need to think hard who that person might be."

James and Antoinette just nodded. They knew she was right and knew also that it may well be someone they knew. That was an extremely uncomfortable thought and they were more disturbed than ever.

Sergeant Fontaine continued. "I need the names of all the guests who attended the opening night. Have you got that information?"

"Yes, definitely. I'll get my assistant, Eleanor, to do it."

"Has anyone been here in the last couple of days who was also here last night?"

"There were some," James answered. "There were caterers, florists, cleaners and a string quartet."

"Then add their details to the guest list. Is there anything you need to ask?" she said, addressing DC Swann.

"You said the painting was insured. Who paid the premium?"

"We did. It was all part of our curating responsibility."

"So what's the situation now that the painting is ostensibly sold?"

"Not sure." James considered the situation. "Probably the responsibility is still ours as it was still here in our gallery."

Such a realisation made Antoinette inwardly groan, understanding the complexity they were now dealing with. Suddenly, there was a noise downstairs, and then a voice calling. "Hi Antoinette. It's me, Della. Shall I come up to the office?"

"It's our cleaner," Antoinette explained.

Sergeant Fontaine responded immediately. "Go down quickly, constable. Explain that there has been an incident but give no details. Ask her to go home but say that we will need to question her later." Then, addressing Antoinette and James, she said "I suggest you do the same with the caterers. Get their details so that we know who they are, and where to question them. Okay?"

"Yes, we'll do that. And what about us? Do we need to leave too?" Antoinette questioned.

"No, but try to keep out of the gallery itself, as it is now a crime scene. I can see you are both still stunned, but I'll need to see you both again. In the meantime, is there anything else you need to tell us?" They both shook their heads, but then James suddenly had a thought.

"There is one thing." he said. "The artist, Raphael, doesn't yet know about the theft."

"Don't worry, we'll let him know. We urgently need to speak to him anyway. Is he staying on the island?"

"Yes, at the Olive Tree."

"Right. Now, don't forget the information I requested. Can your assistant e-mail it to me?"

"Yes, I'm sure she can. I'll get her on to it straight away." Antoinette realised there was another hurdle to cross in explaining things to Eleanor. The immediate future looked somewhat frightening, full of doubt and suspicion, and beset with rumour and problems. Her eyes misted over at the thought.

"We'll be in touch," said Sergeant Fontaine as she moved off, meeting DC Swann downstairs, where he had remained after Della, the cleaner, had gone. He had cast a swift eye over the gallery, but nothing untoward had caught his attention. From the entrance, Sergeant Fontaine shouted back: "Don't forget to keep the gallery completely closed. We'll let you know when to expect the forensics team." Then they were gone.

Antoinette fell into James' arms, "Oh James, what are we going to do? How could this have happened?"

"I don't know, sweetheart. I'm sure the police will do their best, but I have a sinking feeling that we aren't going to get Madrigal back."

* * *

Shortly afterwards, James telephoned Eleanor.

"Hi, James."

"Eleanor, are you due to come into the gallery today?"

"Later, yes. Annie said not to bother until everything was cleared away from last night."

"Could you come in now, do you think? Or as soon as you can? Come straight up to the office."

"Of course I can. Is everything alright? Is it Annie? Is she ill?"

"No, nothing like that. We're both here now. I'll explain when you get here."

Not knowing what else to do, they both hung around the office, but it wasn't long before Eleanor arrived.

"Come straight up, Eleanor."

One look at Antoinette and she knew that all was not well. She looked far away and her eyes were red and puffy. Equally, James looked drained and pale, which was unusual for him. Eleanor was immediately anxious.

"What is it? What's wrong?" she asked, going over to take Antoinette's hand and sitting down beside them both.

It was Antoinette who spoke first. "Eleanor, Madrigal is gone."

"You mean the buyer has taken it already, rather than leaving it until the end of the exhibition?"

"No. Actually, Eleanor, Madrigal has been stolen."

"What do you mean?" said Eleanor turning pale, not quite taking in what she had been told.

James gave her the details. "When Antoinette came in earlier to wait for the cleaners, she saw that Madrigal had gone."

"I can't believe it! How could anyone do that?"

"But they have," confirmed Antoinette, "Whoever it was knew how to turn off the alarm; it had been planned, I'm sure. I wasn't here; I'd stayed over at mum and dad's. But to be honest, even if I had been here, I was so exhausted I daresay I wouldn't have heard anything. But if only I had been here, I might have been able to stop it."

"You don't know that, and how do you know they wouldn't have attacked you? But you said 'they'. Do you mean that you think there was more than one?"

"Oh, no. we're not sure at all about that," answered James. "Anyway, the police have been and we can only hope they take it seriously."

Antoinette then asked her about the guests. "The police want a list of all the guests, staff and musicians who were here last night, along with their contact details, as well as others like the florists and caterers. Could you put the list together for us, and then e-mail it to the police as soon as possible?"

"Of course I will, I'll get on to it now. Do you mean that the police are going to interview everyone who was here? That's a massive job."

"I know. It will take ages I suppose, but I'll get the police contact details for you and then leave you to it. Thanks Eleanor, that's a big help."

"You can do it at home if you wish," James suggested. "I'm taking Annie back to her parents', and then I need to go and tell my family too, especially if the police will want to interview them."

"Before you go, what did Raphael say? I hate to think of his reaction." Eleanor frowned.

"Actually, we haven't spoken to him. The police were going straight to the Olive Tree to tell him and ask some questions. You're right though,

Eleanor, I didn't want to be the person to tell him," echoed James. Antoinette gave a weak smile, knowing she didn't like the idea either.

"I'm still concerned about Constantin too," continued Eleanor. "He didn't turn up at all last night, and I still haven't heard from him. Hopefully, the police will speak to him too, and then we'll find out where he was and how Raphael reacted. I suppose he and Raphael could have argued, quite likely I suppose given Raphael's temperament. Con said he isn't the easiest person to work for, which is a bit of an understatement I would say. It's strange he hasn't contacted me though, no e-mail, no text, or phone call."

"Oh, Eleanor," intercepted Antoinette. "We didn't tell the Police about Constantin. They'll need to speak to him too. How can we have forgotten, especially as we are unsure where he is?"

"But everyone is stressed, you couldn't remember everything." Eleanor reassured her.

"You're right, but we'd better do it now. The Police might think we are holding back information."

"Why would they think that? We just forgot." said James.

Antoinette continued, "Shall I ring them now? Where's that telephone number they gave us?"

Eleanor pointed "It's there, on the coffee table."

Antoinette picked up the card and rang the Police.

"Okay then, I'll go now if you don't need me for anything else. I'll find that information the Police asked for." Eleanor said. She gave James a hug. Antoinette waved.

"Take care Eleanor. Keep the door locked when we go and don't open it unless it's the Police."

"James, you're frightening me now."

"No, don't worry Eleanor, we just want you to be safe."

As she left, Eleanor could hear Antoinette on the phone.

"Sergeant Fontaine speaking. How can I help you?"

"Sergeant, it's Antoinette Duchenne, you've just left our gallery, La Perle."

"Oh, yes, so what can I do for you?"

"Well, you asked us to contact you if we remembered anything."

"Oh, right, go on," said the sergeant, interested now.

"Well, we forgot to tell you about Constantin, he's Raphael's agent, you see. He's been involved with the exhibition from the beginning, a lovely, helpful man. We forgot to mention him as you only asked who was there on the opening night, and Constantin wasn't. In fact, we hadn't seen him for over twenty four hours. We were surprised he didn't come along to the preview and he still hasn't appeared."

"What do you know about this agent?"

"Not a lot, it was simply a business relationship, but he was always kind and helpful. His surname is Patras and he is staying at the Olive Tree, same as Raphael. We rang because we thought you would want to speak to him."

"We certainly do. Thank you for the information Ms Duchenne, we'll be in touch."

Antoinette put the phone down. "Okay?" asked James.

"Yes, but she wasn't very friendly. Anyway, we've done what we needed to do."

Chapter Twelve

The reception and reaction the police received at the Olive Tree was somewhat different from at the gallery. Though small, the hotel was known for its luxury, and Raphael was staying in the third-floor suite. The constable knocked, but it was several minutes before the door opened, and then by only a crack. A dishevelled Raphael, eyes red and blurry, hair awry, was dressed in a bathrobe. Sergeant Fontaine led the conversation.

"Mr Harcourt-Smythe?"

"Yes, that's me. What do you want?" he replied brusquely.

"I am Detective Sergeant Fontaine and my colleague is Detective Constable Swann, from Guernsey police. We'd like to speak with you. Can we come in?"

"It's not convenient."

"Well sir, whether it is convenient or not for you, it's essential for us."

"You can speak to me here, now. I'm sure it won't take long."

"Afraid not sir." Sergeant Fontaine now struggling to control her frustration. "So will you please let us in."

"I don't know, I don't particularly want to speak to the police," he answered truculently.

"Maybe not, sir, but we need to speak to you. It's in your own interest, sir." She was trying her best to control her growing anger at this obstructive person. Then, reluctantly, Raphael opened the door slightly more, giving just enough room for both officers to squeeze through.

"Thank you," said the constable. But Raphael remained extremely solemn and sulky. He had no intention of being cooperative, and all three remained standing in the living area of his suite. The sergeant wasted no time; she was not going to pander to this sulky man.

"You are an artist, I believe?"

Raphael was immediately insulted. "An artist! I am one of the most respected and richest artists in the world, but I wouldn't expect you to know that."

"That's as maybe," replied Sergeant Fontaine, not rising to his insults and totally unimpressed by the man. "You currently have an exhibition at the La Perle gallery here in Guernsey?"

"I do. Look, what is all this about? I'm far too busy and important to waste time like this."

The sergeant looked at Constable Swann, who rolled his eyes. "Sorry you feel like that, sir." Her voice was caustic. "Maybe you will understand when I tell you."

"Oh, good, so you finally get round to it. What is so important that you have to spoil my day? I really need to rest after my wonderful opening yesterday."

"Straight to the point then. I need to tell you that one of your paintings has been stolen."

"What? Are you sure?"

"Of course we're sure. We aren't stupid, sir, even though you seem to think we are. The painting is Madrigal, is that the name? Is that your painting, sir?"

For a moment Raphael was silent, then suddenly let out a high-pitched scream, followed by his dropping to the floor in a dead faint. Constable Swann checked he was okay, and then helped him to his feet. "That was a shock for you, sir," the constable said in a sympathetic tone.

"A shock? A shock?" After a moment's hesitation he screamed again.

"Look, come and sit down," the constable continued, and Raphael let himself be led to the sofa when he literally collapsed into it. Constable Swann sat beside him but the sergeant remained standing. Suddenly, Raphael started laughing hysterically.

"Ten million pounds, ten million pounds," he said and continued to laugh. Then, as his eyes glazed over, the officers realised he had fainted yet again, his head resting on the sofa back.

"Get him a drink, Dean – there must be some whisky or brandy somewhere."

There was, and Dean poured him a large whisky. Raphael was coming round and he sipped the whisky he was offered.

"I can see how upset you are," Sergeant Fontaine said.

"Upset! Upset! Only just a little bit!" Raphael countered sarcastically.

"Then we'll come back and speak to you later. I suggest you calm down and think about what you can tell us. Anything about the events leading up to the theft. We will also need the details of the anonymous buyer, and the amount that was agreed. In the meantime, I believe you have an agent, Mr Constantin Patras? We would also like to speak to him. Is he staying at this hotel?"

"Yes, but not in a suite. That would be a bit too grand for him."

'He may be a famous artist and is understandably upset at the theft, but I am finding it very hard to be patient with him,' Sergeant Fontaine admitted to herself. She glanced at the constable; he rolled his eyes again, and she was relieved he thought the same.

"So, do you know his room number? Perhaps we can ring through and arrange to speak to him?"

"He isn't there," Raphael replied shortly.

"He's gone out? Well, we'll arrange to speak to him when he returns."

"No, I mean he isn't there. I don't know where he is."

"He's your agent, how can you not know where he is?"

Raphael remained stubbornly silent.

"Mr Harcourt-Smythe, we're waiting for an answer."

"I really don't know where he is." Then, after a short period of silence, he reluctantly continued, knowing the officers would continue to question him. "I don't know, because he is no longer my agent."

"And why is that?"

"Because I sacked him on Thursday. We had a big argument. How dare he argue with me? I'm his employer and he should do what I say! I wasn't going to let him speak to me like he did. He was throwing insults at me, so I told him he no longer worked for me."

"What did Mr Patras say to that?"

"Nothing, he just walked off. It doesn't matter, he wasn't a very good agent anyway. I'm better off without him. I'll find someone who recognises what a privilege it is to work for me."

Both officers looked at each other in dismay, thinking 'Is this man for real?'

"Okay, Mr Harcourt-Smythe. We'll be back to speak to you later. Until then, please remain here. If you think of anything, let us know immediately. It's also imperative we find Mr Patras. We would be grateful to know if you hear from him."

Both officers were about to leave when Raphael stood up, as if just remembering something. "I suppose you've spoken to those two gallery owners? I knew I shouldn't have trusted them to host this exhibition. Stupid amateurs, stupid; what was I thinking? Idiots, both of them." He started to wail. The police officers left, relieved to get away.

"Well, that was good, Dean," she said and both laughed, to relieve the tension as much as anything else.

"What an obnoxious man," replied the constable.

"Yes, and a snob, and arrogant," observed Sergeant Fontaine. "We'll have to pin him down next time, though."

"I agree, and we need to find out more about this painting, especially if we want to find it. Apart from it being big, we don't know anything."

"You're right. I'm sure the gallery owners will have details, and hopefully a photograph too. Could you track them down, Dean, and see what you can find out?"

"I'll get on to it right away."

"Before you do, I want to run something past you. I'm concerned about this Constantin Patras. If what the artist says is true, Mr Patras may have been so angry and vengeful that he stole the picture, not necessarily for his personal gain, but to get back at the treatment from his employer. What do you think? It's a definite motive, isn't it?"

The constable agreed. "It certainly fits. It seems a real coincidence that both the painting and Mr Patras disappeared after their argument."

"And remember, he had access to the gallery and probably the alarm too. We may have solved this theft Dean, but unfortunately we haven't a clue where he or the painting is. It's hard to hide a large painting, or to get it off the island. I think we'd better contact the airport and ferries and tell them to maintain extreme vigilance. We'll give them a description of Mr Patras and the painting. So come on, we have no time to waste."

Catastrophe at La Perle
Reporter Daniel West

Owners of La Perle gallery, Antoinette Duchenne and James Kerrissey, both Guernsey residents, are devastated by the theft of a major art installation from their new exhibition by world-famous artist Mr Raphael Harcourt-Smythe. The painting, believed to be worth ten million pounds, was stolen despite state-of-the-art security. It seems that the thief or thieves were able to enter the gallery unseen and unheard. Antoinette, who lives in a flat above the gallery, was away overnight, and so neither saw nor heard anything. Extremely shocked, she told our Herald reporter 'I just can't believe this has happened.' She was too upset to continue. Joint owner, James Kerrissey, also shocked, said 'It is just inconceivable that this should happen'. Mr Harcourt-Smythe, the artist and owner of the painting, was unavailable for comment, but was believed to have been hysterical when informed of the theft by the police.

Anyone with any information regarding the theft is asked to contact Guernsey police. 'This is a serious crime,' the police commented.

Chapter Thirteen

They left Eleanor at the gallery, and James – under some protest – dropped Antoinette at her parents' house. He knew she was better away from La Perle, and Alex and Charles could give her the cossetting she needed just now. By the time James left her, she admitted that she felt more secure and less troubled, even though her parents were, themselves, shocked when they heard what had happened at the gallery. However, they did now know and wouldn't just hear from strangers or the media. It just left James to tell his own parents, but they weren't at the Meribel, so he phoned.

"Hello sweetheart," said Julia, happy to hear from her son. "Oh James, we so enjoyed it last night, except for that horrible Raphael man. He spoiled the whole evening in a way, and poor Georgia was so embarrassed. Luca had been so good – how could he do that in front of all those people? And being drunk was no excuse as far as I am concerned."

"Listen, mum, where are you? I wondered if I could join you. Dad's with you, I assume?"

"Of course he is. We're at the Strawberry Farm, which you recommended to us and it's lovely." Then Julia wondered suddenly if all was well. "Is everything okay, James?"

"Fine, mum. I'll join you at the farm. See you soon."

"Well, that was a strange call," she said to her husband.

"Why? What's so wrong with him wanting to join us for a cuppa?"

"Nothing, it's just that there was something in his voice, Johnny, that's all."

"You've probably imagined it. Just relax and enjoy your son's company."

* * *

109

James got himself a drink when he arrived and went over to join his parents.

"Thought you might have brought Antoinette," Julia said, a little disappointed.

"No, I've left her in Fort George with her parents."

"There's something wrong isn't there, James? Come on, what is it?"

James didn't quite know where to start, so immediately just blurted out the news. "Madrigal was stolen from the gallery last night."

Johnny and Julia were both stunned into silence. They were also confused.

"What? What do you mean? It was there all evening."

"Yes, mum, but it was stolen during the night. Antoinette found out this morning when she went to La Perle."

Julia, understanding the significance of the theft, went pale. Johnny was staring in disbelief.

"But how, James? Why? Yet you can claim the insurance?"

"We'll try, of course. I need to tell you, though, that the police will want to interview you, as they will everyone who attended last night." James looked at their shocked expressions. "Don't worry, they just want to know if you can remember anything that might help, you know, whether you overheard someone talking or whatever."

"Then we'll extend our stay, won't we Johnny?" replied Julia emphatically.

"You don't need to, mum. The police in England can interview you at home."

"No, no! We're staying, son," said Johnny, confirming their decision.

"It isn't just to do with the police. We're not leaving you – we're here to support you. Georgia and Oliver will need to go back, though. I'll speak to them. Now no arguments, James, we'll contact the Meribel now." Julia left no room to convince them otherwise.

"Thank you. I appreciate it." James felt such overwhelming love for them that they had unhesitatingly chosen to stay. He had always both loved and respected his parents. They had always supported and encouraged both him and Georgia. They were not as wealthy as Alex and Charles, but they had made sacrifices to send both of them to private school, and then they had supported him at university so that he had little debt at the end of his studies. Shortly after his graduation, his maternal grandfather had died. Over many years, his grandfather had built up a successful haulage company and sold out so he could retire. Tragically, he died from an undiscovered aneurism just two months later, leaving Julia, Georgia and James as the major beneficiaries of his estate. His parents now lived a comfortable relaxed life, while James had used some of his inheritance to fund the gallery. He had not regretted it, even now, though it would be easy to feel otherwise.

Wanting to calm the situation down, he asked how they liked the Strawberry Farm and he wasn't surprised when they both told him that they liked it very much. He came himself quite often. It was inland, the owners having taken over several abandoned greenhouses, the result of the collapse of tomato growing, a staple crop for Guernsey not too many years ago. A new crop of strawberries now filled the greenhouses and poly-tunnels. A 'pick your own' arrangement brought in many people and it had grown, not just into a farm shop but a café and gift shop too. There were many regulars as well as visitors, and the atmosphere was relaxed. He excused himself and went over to the gift shop, where he bought a strawberry liqueur for Julia and some strawberry gin for Johnny. He wanted them to know that he appreciated their support and both were delighted with their gifts.

* * *

Later that same afternoon, the police were continuing with their interviews, and when they visited Raphael again he was calmer, but a little the worse for drink, though it had mellowed his mood, and he was somewhat more co-operative. He told them he had no idea of who, or why, anyone would steal his painting.

"Of course, it was magnificent. Perhaps someone was upset that it had been sold when they had wanted it for themselves." Then he briefly described Madrigal, explaining that it wasn't a painting in the traditional sense, more of an installation. Continuing his testimony, he explained that he had left the gallery late at night. "I was exhausted, as you can imagine. I came straight back here and slept all night."

"Do you have an alibi, sir?" asked constable Swann.

"Afraid not, but I truly was here all night."

Sergeant Fontaine had become convinced that Raphael's angry agent was the one involved in the theft and decided there was no need to continue with the interview. She said to herself 'He's obnoxious, but I'm more interested in Mr Patras.' She nodded to Dean, who understood her thoughts.

"Alright Mr Harcourt-Smythe, we'll leave you now. But if you come across any information about the theft please let us know immediately." She handed him her card with details of how to contact her. "Please do not leave the island. Do you understand?"

"Yes, I understand. Now please, leave me alone."

* * *

Over the next few days, many of the guests from the exhibition were interviewed, some by the police in both England and France. But progress was slow and little was learned. Everyone spoken to seemed only to remember that Madrigal was still in place when they left the gallery late in the evening. Most also remembered that the painting had been sold and were curious as to who the buyer was, and what amount had been paid. Raphael had stubbornly refused to disclose any information.

The gallery remained closed. James and Antoinette were at something of a loose end, waiting for news. There seemed to be no answers. Eleanor had worked hard putting together all the information for the police, but Antoinette noticed that she was abnormally quiet and clearly distraught. Cajoling her, Antoinette encouraged her to explain what was wrong.

"Constantin is still missing, and I'm really concerned about him," she told her, close to tears. "I'm sure something has happened to him. He would have let me know what was happening otherwise, I know he would."

Antoinette shared her concern, but there was nothing she could do to relieve her acute anxiety.

One thing was for sure, however, was that Raphael was conspicuous by his absence. Antoinette wondered why, but she was also relieved. The last thing she and James needed was Raphael with his hysterics. They were hysterical enough themselves. The only thing they wanted to ask him was who had bought the painting, and what had he done about contacting the purchaser. They would survive in ignorance for the time being though; it was preferable to dealing with Raphael.

* * *

Janice Fontaine had lived all her life in Guernsey, but had had periods of training on Jersey and on the English mainland. Nothing had convinced her that life was better anywhere other than her beloved Guernsey. She acknowledged that career opportunities were not great; the whole island force was only small, and homicide and violent crime were thankfully uncommon. Nevertheless, she had become a detective sergeant and crime was varied enough. She had no regrets about staying on Guernsey. None of her family had ever been associated with the police force, but she had known from a young age that she wanted to be a police officer, and, undeterred, she had fulfilled her ambition. Now in her forties, she was content; happily married to a Guernsey man who was a schoolteacher; they had two daughters she was proud of and had fortunately never given her cause for concern. Nowhere was perfect, and neither was Guernsey, but she knew it was safer and better than many places. It was a good place to bring up children, and was a place of beautiful beaches, where she loved to spend time with her family when she could. Neither tall nor well built, she nevertheless had determination and a presence which was respected by her colleagues. Yet never before had she had to deal with such a strange case. She was, of course, familiar with working with the many visitors to the island, but this case presented unique problems. Art theft was not an uncommon crime, though her own limited knowledge told her that it mostly involved international specialist art thieves, who targeted famous, valuable paintings to order that were often never recovered. They were generally clever, skilled, professional thieves and it was worth their while when so much monetary reward was at stake. But where was the motivation for this theft? She sat at her desk and pondered the whole scenario. Who took it, why and what was the reward? She couldn't see the logic for it. Granted, Harcourt-Smythe was well known, but the stolen painting had not been seen in public before and its value was unproven. There seemed to her to be only one logical answer. Constantin Patras was missing. He had been agent and assistant to Harcourt-Smythe. He knew the painting, helped install it, had access to, and knowledge of, the alarm system at La Perle. He had argued with his employer and had been sacked as a result. So, he may have been grossly insolent, or furious that he had been unjustly sacked. Either way, he had walked away and not been seen since. It seemed a perfect opportunity for revenge; to steal the painting that was so important to Harcourt-Smythe. It may have been totally unplanned and done in anger, but as a motive it made some sense. So, where was Patras, and where was the painting? Despite high vigilance at the airport and ferry terminals, he seemed to have disappeared without trace.

'I need to find him,' she told herself. 'Where could he go?' She was determined to find as much information as possible, even though so far no-one seemed to know much about him at all. 'I'll interview the gallery owners again, including their assistant Eleanor. She had been very friendly with Patras and was convinced he would never do such a thing. Yet how long had she known him, and how well had she known him?'

* * *

"Thank you for making yourselves available," said the sergeant as James and Antoinette responded to her request for more questioning. They had been relieved that it was to be at La Perle and not the police station. "There are a few extra questions I need to ask you. It seems formal I know, but it is normal practice." As she spoke, Constable Swann arrived too. "Now, just to clarify a few facts, are you the sole owners of the gallery?"

"Yes, but we have a couple of employees – Eleanor our assistant and Della the cleaner. Then there's Maria and Kate who run the café," responded Antoinette.

"This may seem a little impertinent, but I imagine opening and running such a professional gallery is an expensive enterprise." James and Antoinette looked at each other, both wondering what was coming next. "Was there anyone else originally who may now hold a grudge against you, or perhaps you owe money to?"

Neither were happy with these questions and James answered with barely concealed emotion and growing anger.

"We have no debts and no sleeping partners. Everything we do here is honest and above board."

Undeterred, Sergeant Fontaine carried on. "So where did the money come from to start the business?"

James bristled and Antoinette quickly stepped in to answer.

"Do you really need to know?"

Unabashed, the sergeant continued. "I wouldn't ask otherwise. I realise that it may not seem relevant to you, but I'm just trying to get some background; so will you please answer the question."

James spluttered, but calmly Antoinette answered her.

"James invested most of the money, and still pays bills and wages when there are cash flow issues, although it's less often now as the gallery is turning much better profit."

"Your parents are wealthy, I believe, Miss Duchenne. Did they have any input?"

"What is all this? I don't understand the need for these questions – they are very intrusive."

"Look I'm simply trying to ascertain whether or not anyone else is or has been involved in the gallery and who is perhaps disgruntled, feeling cut out, misled, or whatever and may have a grudge, strong enough to take revenge and steal the painting?"

"You could have explained that before," replied an exasperated Antionette. "The answer, since you seem to know so much about my family, is yes. My family are and always have been supportive to both me and my brother. They gave me a substantial amount to buy the warehouse. But it was a gift, not an investment, they didn't want to be partners or have any involvement in the running of the business. James paid for the conversion."

"Thank you," she said and smiled, the atmosphere now feeling less hostile. "I'm sorry if all this seems intrusive but it is my job and remember I don't need to spy into your family affairs. Like you, Ms Duchenne, I was born and raised here. It's a small island and as you know not much is private. Now before we leave, I'd like to ask a few questions about Mr Patras, who as you are aware has now been missing for several days. Can you both repeat for me the last time you saw him?"

"You go first, James."

James began. "On Friday, the day of the opening, we realised that we hadn't seen him at all that day."

"Who is *we?*"

"Oh right, well essentially Antionette, Eleanor and myself. During the evening, Eleanor approached each of us to ask if we had seen him, and we realised we hadn't. That was important because of all the days, that was the one where we would really have expected him to be there. After all the preparation, this was the pinnacle and we were all proud and wanted to celebrate our success. When we thought about it, we realised we hadn't seen him probably since Thursday, or even Wednesday, when the paintings were displayed."

"Is that your memory too, Antoinette?"

"It is. I mean, it was such an incredibly busy time, I'm not sure I would have missed him at all on Friday if it hadn't been for Eleanor's query. The gallery was packed to capacity. There was also food and music; you can imagine it. To be honest, I think the three of us just assumed he was there."

"What was your impression of Mr Patras?"

Antionette was the first to reply. "Well, I didn't know him well and had never met him before he became involved with the exhibition. But what we do know of him I liked. He was kind, helpful, serene, and he immediately put us at our ease when we first embarked on the planning. You need to understand that we had never undertaken anything like this before. We were uncertain and nervous. Yet from the very beginning he reassured us that all would be well."

"Did you know him any better, James?"

"I very much concur with Annie. He always kept in the background if Raphael was there, but he often came to Guernsey alone to represent Raphael, and on those occasions he was confident and friendly. He was very easy to get along with, but he never really disclosed anything about himself, so I don't even know where he lived or anything. There again, I never asked. It was a pleasant business arrangement I suppose, but no more than that. Eleanor may know a little more than us. They liked each other, but if they did have a more involved relationship, they were very discreet."

"Did you ask Mr Harcourt-Smythe about Mr Patras when you realised he wasn't there?"

"I did." This was James. "He was very drunk, but he did admit that he knew Constantin wasn't there. I asked him why, but in his usual Raphael fashion he wouldn't tell me. I think he said something like – 'What has it to do with you? I'm his employer' – all a bit vague, but he wasn't terribly coherent."

"I think that's all for now, unless Constable Swann has any questions?"

"Just one, Sergeant. Addressing you both, would you say Mr Harcourt-Smythe liked his agent, and conversely what did Mr Patras think of his employer?"

Looking at each other, James nodded and was the first to answer. "Phew, that's a hard one. I would have to say that I have no idea. It was next to impossible to know what Raphael thought, and even harder to know if he liked anybody. He was very arrogant and superior. I believe that the only person he liked was himself. I don't think anyone came up to his expectations. Constantin was always patient and respectful, at least as far as I could see. It can't have been easy working for Raphael – he is such a volatile character. What we saw is only an impression, but if I had to give an opinion, I don't think they liked each other but managed, somehow, to operate a working relationship."

"My opinion very much matches James'. Raphael was always 'on show' and always projected his image of greatness. He did have some charisma but, unfortunately, he was also rude, moody and arrogant, which weren't very endearing traits. I can't imagine he ever stopped to think whether he liked Constantin. Yet Constantin was expert in 'managing' Raphael with all his moods, anxieties and exuberance. Whether he liked him, I don't know but I doubt it. I noticed how, on some occasions, Raphael would make sure Constantin was clearly his 'minion', which was why, as James said, he often kept in the background."

Inwardly Antionette flinched. She knew how easy it could be to be taken in by Raphael, and she was ashamed of the affection she had felt, contradicting James and others about his character. She now realised that his attentions had been insincere and she didn't want to think too deeply about it. What she did know was that, if it hadn't been for Raphael, she may never have realised her true feelings for James, and for that she was grateful.

They were both shattered when the police left.

"Good grief, James, I'd hate to think how you would be treated if you really were a criminal. I felt guilty and hadn't done anything wrong."

They both laughed. "Come on," she continued, "let's go and get a drink somewhere quiet and try to get our thoughts together as to what the police sergeant was thinking." And regarding that, Antoinette didn't like her thoughts and was afraid to voice them.

L'Ancresse was a large expansive sandy beach. They hoped it would be relatively quiet, which it was. At the edge of the beach was a small café which had been there for years. Hardly more than a hut, there were no fancy coffees served here, but Antionette knew that the old-fashioned pots of loose tea and home-made apple pie made up for the café itself, which definitely needed an upgrade. It was traditional, a feature of an older Guernsey, and the view from the window where they sat was beautiful. Antoinette was itching to say what was on her mind but waited until they had been served.

"How are things, Susan?" she asked the waitress, whom she had known for many years. Indeed, Susan sometimes helped with catering for the gallery.

"Not bad Antoinette, but how are you? I was so sorry to hear about your gallery theft; is there any news yet?"

"Afraid not, no. In fact we've just been interviewed by the police again. We just hope that there will be some progress soon."

"Well, I'll get your tea and apple pie."

Antoinette smiled at Susan, who already knew what they would order. Once served, Susan disappeared behind the counter and James poured the tea.

"I think they suspect Constantin," he said, before Antionette had the chance to speak. She was relieved but upset too that both of them had come to the same conclusion. She didn't like to think that Constantin was responsible, but the facts seemed to point that way.

"You're right, I think they do. It's awful, and hard to accept from what we know about him. But are the police right?"

"I don't know, Annie, but I can see where the police are coming from."

"And to be honest what do we really know about him?"

"Not much I suppose," replied James, realising an uncomfortable truth. "We met a pleasant man who seemed sincere and kind, for just a few weeks. Beyond that we have no idea about him."

"I don't want to think it's him, it seems almost disloyal. And what about Eleanor? She'll be devastated, and I don't think she will believe any of it."

"Of course, the biggest question," continued James, "is where is he? If he isn't responsible, why hasn't he turned up to defend himself?"

Perhaps the police were right, but both were hesitant to think it.

* * *

Next morning Sergeant Fontaine was late for work, something she hated. Her daughter Hannah had been violently sick during the night, and wasn't well enough for school. Janice had to quickly find someone to be with her at home. She tried not to appear flustered as she walked into the interview room where Constable Swann and Eleanor were waiting for her. Janice was grateful for her short, straight hair, easily controlled with a quick brush. However, she couldn't hide her tiredness, her hazel eyes smudged with redness. She sat down hastily.

"Thank you for coming in, Ms Grant. We have a few questions to ask you and hope you can clarify some of the things that happened at La Perle." Janice managed a tired smile. "I believe you are a student?"

"I am and coming up to my final year. I was on a placement at La Perle, which became a part-time job. I have managed to secure an internship at the Courtauld Institute in London. I hope to work in the art field or the media. Working at the gallery has really taught me a lot."

"Do you like Ms Duchenne and Mr Kerrissey?"

"Of course, they are both wonderful and I love every minute of my job."

"Now, can you tell us what you remember of the day and evening of the opening night at La Perle?"

"Well, it was hectic all day of course, and Antionette, James and I were there all day. The painting, Madrigal, had been displayed, I think, the day before, and looked great. It was certainly the star of the show. Raphael, I seem to remember, took the day off as a rest day, so we didn't see him until the evening. Everything was ready on time and the gallery looked gorgeous. The official opening was 7pm but James had invited family and close friends to come for 6.30pm as a special preview treat. It gave us some time to spend with them; we knew that when everyone arrived we would be completely run off our feet, which we were. At the end of the evening some of the paintings had been sold. Then the red dot appeared on Madrigal and everyone was really excited. Raphael, of course, wouldn't say who had bought it, nor for how much, and he appeared to have dealt with the sale personally. It was just like Raphael to make a big mystery out of it, but he did say the buyer wanted to remain anonymous, so it made sense."

"Thank you. Could you now tell us a bit about Mr Patras? I understand you and he had become good friends, and you probably know him better than anyone else at La Perle."

Eleanor blushed, then said nervously "What do you want to know?"

"Well, we know he wasn't at the very important opening. Wasn't that a bit strange, seeing it was the culmination of everyone's hard work?"

"Yes, it was strange, which is why I asked Antoinette and James if they had seen him."

"He never turned up, though, did he?"

"No, and I haven't seen or heard from him since, which I just don't understand. He would have told me, I'm sure, if he wasn't going to come for some reason."

"Would you say he was an honest and truthful man, Ms Grant?"

"Definitely." Eleanor was beginning to feel upset and uncomfortable, wondering where the questions were leading. "Really, he was such a lovely man, kind and thoughtful."

"How did he get on with Mr Harcourt-Smythe? Did he like him? Did he enjoy working for him?"

The questions seemed relentless to Eleanor. She was struggling, she had never been to a police station before and the questions were disconcerting, especially since she was really worried about Constantin.

"Constantin was respectful and loyal to Raphael, but in private, when we were together, he admitted that, although he loved the job itself, he was finding it hard to continue working with Raphael. We have all learned over these last months how difficult he can be. He's unpredictable, moody and sometimes very bad tempered. So I understand what Constantin meant, but he was reluctant to leave until after the exhibition. He…" and Eleanor hesitated, not sure if she could carry on.

"What was it you were going to say, Ms Grant? You were going to tell me something else, I think."

"I didn't want to break a confidence that Constantin had told me." Eleanor was close to tears.

"Ms Grant," the sergeant continued softly, "I know he is your friend, and that you wish to remain loyal to him. Breaking a confidence is not easy, but this is a police investigation and we need to know as much as possible. So can you tell us please."

"That's just it," Eleanor blurted out. "I don't know what it means and if it's relevant."

All three were silent.

"Constable Swann, do you think you could go and get us all some coffee while Ms Grant calms down a little." He got up and left, understanding that it might be easier if the sergeant was alone with her. "I know all this is difficult for you and that you are worried about your friend."

"I am," Eleanor answered truthfully, "but I will tell you what he said. Constantin rang on Thursday evening and said that the day before the opening, Raphael was very drunk, and with his defences down, he told Constantin a secret. He was absolutely shocked and angry at what he told him, and when Raphael boasted and laughed at his own cleverness, Constantin was disgusted with him. Then Raphael sobered up and realised what he had admitted. Rather than being angry with himself, he was furious with Constantin, which was typical of Raphael. I'd never known them to argue, but they did that night. I was upset for him, and said we'd talk about it next day at the gallery. But I never saw him again."

"And you have no idea what Raphael told him?"

"No, none at all. Constantin just wouldn't tell me."

"Okay, I think that's all for now, Ms Grant. Thank you for your co-operation."

"You mean I can go now?"

"Yes, of course you can."

Eleanor had never been as relieved as she had been to get away from that place, and sincerely hoped she would never have to go back again. It had been a horrible experience and she desperately needed to speak to someone for reassurance. Yet she was too upset and worked up. She wandered around the town and then found a seat in Liberation Square to think things through. She didn't like her conclusions, she didn't like them at all. 'The police suspect Con. Oh Con, the police think you stole the painting. Where are you? Please come back and prove them wrong,' she said to herself. She became very agitated. 'I won't believe you did it, Constantin, but where are you?'

Back in the interview room, the coffee arrived after Eleanor had left, and Janice brought Constable Swann up to speed. "So what do you think, Dean? Am I on the right track?"

"It seems the most likely scenario to me, and the fact that he's disappeared makes it even more suspicious."

"But what if it's too straightforward?"

"I think your instincts are right and, quite honestly, there aren't any other suspects, are there?"

"So, it's time to speak to the inspector then."

She telephoned and asked if Inspector Louvaine could spare her a few minutes so she could outline her theory and appraise him of the details of the investigation. Inspector Louvaine was a gruff man, but he was well liked and always willing to listen. In his fifties, he had spent all his professional career with Guernsey police. He was thankful the island wasn't a hot bed of crime, but he had gained insight and intuition and was respected for it. Few other officers knew Guernsey and its crime profile better than he. Also, he liked Sergeant Fontaine and respected her judgement. Once slim, he had filled out in middle age, but he was still a handsome man who prided himself on his dress and was known for his expensive suits.

"Can I come in, sir?" Janice queried.

"Come in and take a seat and let's talk about this case."

The sergeant recounted all that she had found out or surmised, and of her conclusion that Mr Constantin Patras was quite likely to have been the person who stole Madrigal, stressing it may not have been pre-meditated, but was possibly an act of revenge.

"So what do you want to do, sergeant?"

"I'd like to officially register him as a suspect and widen our search."

"What did the search of the gallery show? Any fingerprints?"

"Oh, lots of them, sir, but nothing that particularly points to Mr Patras. He's been all over that gallery for months now, and there were hundreds of people at the opening."

"Alright, so what do you need to do? Bear in mind though that this is only a suspicion so far. Keep an open mind, this case is far from conclusive, but I agree it's a logical route to follow."

"We've already alerted the airport and ferries, but so far there have been no sightings. He seems to have disappeared into thin air."

"Sergeant, Guernsey is an island full of boats, yachts and huge liners. There are many ways he could have left the island."

"That's true, sir, I'll get on them. In the case of the boats, will we have to inspect them all, sir?"

"Where you can, Sergeant, yes. You can use some other officers if you think it will help. Remember, though, that yachts come and go all the time, so it won't be easy."

"Yes sir, I realise that." Her heart sank at the overwhelming task in front of her.

"Good luck, Sergeant."

"Thank you, sir." But all she could think about was that he could be miles away from Guernsey by now.

Report from the Guernsey Herald

Visiting Art Agent Missing
Reporter Daniel West

Concern is growing about the whereabouts and safety of Mr Constantin Patras, who has now been missing for several days. As agent for Raphael Harcourt-Smythe, world-famous artist, he has been in Guernsey periodically over the last few months, preparing for an exhibition of Mr Harcourt-Smythe's work at La Perle gallery. He has been missing since he failed to attend the opening of the exhibition, an event very important to him after many months of preparation. The police are eager to eliminate Mr Patras from suspicion of the theft of the star exhibit, estimated to be worth ten million pounds.

Mr Patras is described as tall, with slightly curly dark hair, deep brown eyes, a partially grown beard and of slim and smart appearance. Anyone who thinks they may have seen Mr Patras, or has any information, please contact Guernsey police.

It wasn't just local papers interested in the case: social media, love it or hate it, didn't take any time at all before it was discussing and publicising the story. The Channel Island Life website was inundated with comments, questions and opinions, most of which were unhelpful to the police. Nor was being in the spotlight good for the gallery either. James and Antoinette felt very exposed.

Chapter Fourteen

James, Antoinette and Eleanor were still at something of a loose end. They had been advised to keep the gallery closed, even the café. It was good advice. They knew it was a way of keeping people at bay, knowing that they could not have coped with continual reporters, as well as inquisitive locals and visitors. As much as they understood how interesting it was to everyone else, they just wanted everything solved, desperately wishing that they could return to some semblance of normality. But what was normal anymore? And it was frustrating that the investigation didn't seem to be getting very far. There had been no sightings of Constantin, nor the stolen painting. As for Raphael, he hadn't made a single appearance at the gallery, and Antoinette wondered about his state of mind. After all, he had been robbed of ten million pounds. Or had he? There was still no clue as to who had bought it, or for how much. Nor was she sure about insurance, and what they should do with his other paintings, still hanging in the gallery. Three had been sold, and she didn't know what to do about those either. Like him or not, she needed to speak to Raphael, but when she rang the Olive Tree the manager didn't know where he was. There was no answer from his room and his mobile seemed to be dead.

James' parents, however, despite the unpleasant reason for it, were very much enjoying their unexpectedly extended holiday. Julia had become close to Alex; Charles and Johnny equally so, enjoying a few fishing trip;, whilst Julia and Alex had become ladies who lunch, and there was no shortage of lovely eating places. One day, for a change, they walked from Alex's house in Fort George, a prestigious residential area, along the cliffs to a restaurant above Fermain Bay. They were windblown by the time they arrived and were glad to rest on the terrace with a glass of wine. It was a clear day with far-reaching views, and Julia pointed to an island in the distance.

"That's Herm," explained Alex. "We can go there one day. It's small but lovely, with no cars and just one hotel. I was about to say that it is also peaceful, but it can get very busy at this time of year. There are regular ferries there these days, but you know at one time you had to get up very early and go with the milk boat."

Julia laughed, trying to imagine a former Guernsey. "Was life here simpler then?"

Alex thought before answering. "In some ways, yes, but the harsh brutality of the German Occupation in World War Two was a horrible period. Times have moved on, but there are still so many reminders here from that time."

Julia shivered. "It must have been awful. I'm not sure how one copes with something like that."

They needed to speak of lighter topics, the gallery too being off limits, especially the news about Constantin Patras being the main suspect.

"So, what do you think about James and Antoinette?" Julia asked. "Has she said anything to you, Alex?"

"No, but I know what you are thinking, and I agree with you. They are certainly different, holding hands and smiling at each other knowingly. It's difficult when they are both under so much stress."

"That's true but despite that, I can see a change in James. He has loved Antoinette for so long now, I really do hope they have finally realised how much they mean to each other."

Alex agreed. "I hope so too. Antoinette seemed so unaware of his feelings and I think it was this crisis that caused a sea change."

"It's wonderful news," added Julia earnestly. Then, when she went for another glass of wine for them both, she intended bringing the menu too; the walk and fresh sea air had given her quite an appetite.

* * *

Alex picked up a copy of the local paper which had been left on another table. She normally read the paper and listened to the local news, but so much had been happening that she had missed recent editions. However, there was a report which intrigued her.

Body Discovered on Local Beach
Reporter Daniel West

The body of a man, believed to have been washed ashore on the tide, was discovered on Vazon beach. A local resident was walking his dog and found the body. "It was an awful sight," said Mr Andrew Bouteille of St Martins. "My dog started barking and running across the sand. It was the last thing I expected when I caught up with him and realised he had run towards a body. I felt sick and faint and thought what a terrible thing to happen to someone."

Police say it is too early for an identification as the body had been in the sea for several days. "But we are working diligently to identify him," commented Inspector Louvaine of St Peter Port police.

Alex pointed the article out to Julia when she returned. "That's tragic. I suppose he could have fallen from a yacht."

"Very likely," agreed Alex. "But it could also be a surfer who got caught in the undercurrent."

"What makes you think that?"

"Well, because Vazen beach is very popular with surfers. It's sometimes crowded with them at weekend when the waves are singing."

"Could well be then," agreed Julia, ready to order her meal.

* * *

When Alex next spoke to her daughter, she told her about the body. Antoinette hadn't read the article either, but, like many Guernsey residents, they were both keen to keep up with the Guernsey gossip. Neither knew many surfers, but if it was a yachtsman, both Alex and Charles would be interested in his identity. Alex would keep an eye out for when the man was identified, hoping he wasn't from Guernsey, and especially that it wasn't a person they knew.

* * *

As hoped, there was soon a further report in the next newspaper edition. It was highlighted too, on local radio and channel TV. However, it was not the news that Alex, Julia and Antoinette were expecting.

Vazon Body Identified
Reporter Daniel West

> *Further information about the identity of the body washed up on Vazon beach has been released by police. Detective Sergeant Fontaine said, "We now believe that the body is that of Mr Constantin Patras, who has been missing for many days. We are awaiting a formal identification, but, nevertheless, we are confident that it is Mr Patras. We can confirm that his body had been in the water for several days before being washed ashore. Further investigations are in place to ascertain the cause of death". Further questions were asked but the police had no further details to disclose and the mystery surrounding his death remains.*

Antoinette could not believe what she was reading, but tuning in to the local radio told the same story. She reached James on his mobile. He was at the Meribel with his parents, enjoying their company and was more relaxed than he had been for days. When Antoinette told him the news, he was very quiet.

"I can't believe it, Annie, but the police are sure, are they?"

"They must be. I don't think they would release his name otherwise."

"But he hasn't been formally identified, so how can they be sure?"

"Maybe he had some identification on him. I don't know James, but it is so awful. Poor Constantin. What is happening here? And what have we got ourselves into?"

"I don't know Annie, I don't know."

Then Antoinette realised something else. "What about Eleanor? She must know by now. I can't imagine how she is reacting – it is such a terrible experience for a young woman. I'm going to go and see her, James. I'll speak to you later."

"I'll wait here at the Meribel," James said.

Julia and Johnny had been relaxing in the lounge with James and heard the anguish in his voice.

"Darling, is everything alright?"

"No not really, mum." Johnny too was alert and listening. "Do you remember reading about a body being found on a beach?"

"Of course, Alex and I were discussing it when we were out for lunch."

"Well, the police have identified it as being Constantin. He has been missing, do you remember?"

"Of course we do," both answered, almost in unison.

"Oh James, I'm so sorry, for Constantin, you and Antoinette," Julia said as she hugged her son.

"It isn't good, is it?" continued James. "What have we become involved in here? We were so excited about the exhibition, and it turns out like this. And the gallery, what will this do to our reputation? I feel so guilty about Constantin, and still can't believe he was involved in the theft. But what on earth was he doing to get himself drowned?"

"I don't know," Julia replied. "But you have to believe that the police will get to the bottom of it all. As for the gallery, people have short memories, you know. Don't worry – it will be fine, honestly."

"I hope so mum, I really hope so." Yet he couldn't convince himself that it would be.

* * *

James caught up with Antoinette later at her flat. She had been right about Eleanor.

"She's taken it really badly, as you would imagine – she's so shocked and poorly. Her mum told me that when Eleanor heard the news she almost fainted, then dashed to the bathroom and was sick. She's still very shaken and her mum has sent her to bed. I didn't want to disturb her, so I left some flowers and came home. I do hope she will be okay. I feel quite responsible for her and a bit guilty too."

"But why? That's silly, Annie, and you know it. Eleanor knows it was not your fault and so do you."

"You're right, but this whole scenario is turning into a nightmare. Can it get any worse, do you think?"

"I hope not, I really do hope not. Come here." He gave her a tender embrace. "We can at least comfort each other," he said quietly.

"Don't leave me tonight, James, I don't want to be alone. Just for tonight, let's try and forget the mess we are in and enjoy being together."

Chapter Fifteen

The phone call asking Sergeant Fontaine to go to the morgue had certainly taken her by surprise. The pathologist told her that he had found something unexpected when he performed the post-mortem on Mr Patras. She and Detective Constable Swann quickly made their way. She was still convinced that he was the thief, his death simply an unfortunate consequence, presumably occurring when he was trying to escape. She was shocked when the pathologist explained his findings. Robert Fordson was the senior pathologist and wasn't known to make mistakes.

"Thank you for coming down so quickly," he said. They were all three in his office whilst he explained his findings. "I'm afraid the death of this man is not straightforward."

Sergeant Fontaine sighed. "What's the problem then?" she asked.

"Firstly, he didn't drown. There is no indication of water in his lungs. I would say he was dead before he hit the water."

"So, do you know what killed him? Was it an accident?"

"Yes, I think I do know how he died but no, I don't think it was accidental."

"What then?" asked Janice as she pushed the pathologist to disclose what he knew.

"Come on, I'll show you." All three headed to the morgue, never a pleasant place, and donned masks and coverings before walking over to where the body lay.

Constable Swann, still unused to such procedures, did not want to get too close. He hung back, hoping his sergeant would not object. The pathologist drew their attention to his head, which was the crucial evidence. "Can you see the wound here, on the back of his head? It's a massive gash, most likely the result of being hit by a heavy blunt instrument."

"Couldn't it just be the result of him hitting a rock or something when he fell into the sea?" asked the sergeant, who was looking for an easier solution.

"It could, but it isn't. It's my professional opinion that this man was murdered. Furthermore, it isn't the only injury. There are signs that he was stabbed; not severe enough to have killed him, but clear enough to suggest evidence of a fight or scuffle. He tried to defend himself, but it was the massive blow which killed him."

"That throws my theory to the wind. Thank you, Robert." Janice Fontaine was not a happy woman.

"I'm sorry, but I can only tell you the truth."

"Yes, I know," she conceded.

She and the constable drove back to the office, an uncomfortable silence between them. She wasn't normally a moody person and DC Swann generally found her easy to work with. Not today though. She was clearly furious, going into her office and slamming the door behind her. The constable left her to it, and went for a cup of coffee, contemplating all he had just learned and what it meant.

Forced to reconsider her original thoughts, the sergeant calmed herself, determined to solve what was turning into a very strange crime, in fact two crimes now. However much she thought, she remained puzzled. She was convinced Patras was the thief but if so, why was he murdered? Did he have someone working with him? And where was the painting? Did an accomplice kill him and make off with the goods? If so, then who on earth could it be? Perhaps I'm on the wrong track altogether, she thought. I need to re-think. If I assume instead that Patras wasn't the thief, then who was, and why was Patras killed? Did he know who had stolen Madrigal and been murdered because of it? That's possible, but who could he have seen with the painting and where? Also, the thief apparently needed to have known how to get in and out of the gallery. And is the painting still on the island? Has Patras hidden it? If not, then the thief must have been able, somehow, to spirit it away. And if it isn't still on the island, how was it smuggled out? By private yacht maybe, but then everyone who saw the painting confirmed how large it was. Also, there are hundreds of yachts here, and even more when visitors sail in and then sail off elsewhere. Janice was annoyed and frustrated with herself. 'I really thought I had solved this case, and then it comes back with a vengeance to haunt me. I certainly don't want to have to check every yacht in the marina, and how can I check the ones which have come and gone?' She knew she would have to consult with her inspector, reluctant though she was to do it. She didn't like the idea of having to admit that her suspicions might well have been wrong. Worse still, this was now a murder case, and the inspector might well take over the investigation, leaving her out in the cold. She decided to give herself some thinking time. She could leave the office and be uncontactable, so if her inspector wanted to speak to her, he couldn't – at least for a while. Popping her head round the constable's office door, she told him she was going out. Constable Swann was surprised when she wouldn't say where she was going.

"Where shall I say you are, if you're needed?" he asked.

"Say you don't know and that I had to dash out and wasn't sure when I would be back." She quickly disappeared before he could ask any more questions. He shook his head and got on with his work, hoping that he wouldn't have to explain anything to his bosses.

* * *

Janice almost dragged Detective Constable Swann out of his seat when she returned sometime later.

"Come on, Dean, get to the car."

"Where are we going?"

"I'll tell you when we're on our way," she said, hurrying to the car. Janice seemed to have energised herself and once on their way, she said "I don't have any real new theories, but we must carry on. We are going to interview all the relevant people again. Someone, somewhere, has a clue to what happened, even if they don't realise it."

Constable Swann looked at her and groaned to himself. He wasn't convinced but had no choice but to concur.

"So, we will tease the information out of them," she said confidently. "First stop is the Olive Tree to speak again to Mr Smythe." The constable groaned again; he couldn't stand the man. "He's been keeping a remarkably low profile, which doesn't seem in keeping with what we've seen of him, nor the views of those who knew him better," she continued.

Dean conceded that she was probably right but was unsure how co-operative he would be. "There may well be something he isn't telling us, deliberately or not."

Approaching reception, the sergeant asked to speak to the manager and explained they wanted to speak to Mr Harcourt-Smythe.

"I'll ring through to his room, but I'm not sure of a response. None of the staff have seen him for a few days, nor has he ordered any food from room service, which is his usual practice." As expected, there was no reply, and it was the same when his room was contacted a second time.

"You're sure he hasn't checked out?"

"Yes, I'm sure," the manager replied. "If he has, he has left without paying his bill. But, as far as we are aware, he is still registered as a resident here."

"Do you have a pass key to his room?"

"Yes, of course, Sergeant. Would you like me to accompany you? "The manager asked obligingly.

"Thank you, that would be great." The constable followed at a quick pace.

The manager knocked on the room door, more from habit rather than the expectation of a reply. After a short pause, the sergeant asked for the door to be opened.

"Thank you, Ms Rodrigues," said the constable as he looked at the manager's name-badge and gave an appreciative smile.

As expected, Harcourt-Smythe was nowhere in his suite, which was dishevelled. Given the 'Do not disturb' sign on the door, the cleaners hadn't been near for a while. A quick search told them he had gone. His suitcase, computer, phone and some clothes had gone with him. He had left everything else in disarray. The television was switched on with low volume, an attempt to make it seem as if the room was occupied.

"Damn!" Janice said under her breath. "So where is he?" she asked to no-one in particular. "He was told not to leave either the hotel or the island. If he intended to, then he should have let the police know. Constable, go back downstairs with the manager. I want you to interview every member of staff to find out who had any contact with Mr Harcourt-Smythe, when they last saw him, and if they have any information about him. Anything, even if they think it's irrelevant, is useful at this point."

After they had left, Janice took time to look around for clues, even though she believed there was nothing to find, nor any hint of where he'd gone or when. She knew he had left and wasn't coming back to this hotel. Again, she was furious. A vital witness had disappeared, and what did that mean?

* * *

Next day, police issued a bulletin, once again requesting information about a missing person. Inspector Louvain released a statement which was sent to radio, TV and newspapers across the Channel Islands.

> *Police are seeking information about a visitor to Guernsey, Mister Raphael Harcourt-Smythe, who has been a frequent visitor over recent months and has most recently been staying at the Olive Tree. It is vital that we question him and we would be grateful for anyone who has any information regarding his whereabouts to contact the police immediately.*
>
> *Mister Harcourt-Smythe may have information about another missing person and we need to contact him. Mister Harcourt-Smythe is described as being of medium height, slim build, late thirties, clean shaven, with blue/grey eyes and blond hair which is possibly dyed. Smythe is known for his flamboyant dress, his clothes colourful and distinctive. Photographs, along with an emergency number, are to be distributed across the island.*

If James and Antoinette thought things couldn't get any worse, then they were both wrong. Just two days later, the police announced that they were treating Constantin's death as suspicious, and two days after that they declared that he had, in fact, been murdered, although details of his death were not released. What the police did say was that, in the light of this murder and possible link with the art theft, their investigation would be stepped up. They clearly thought that the two crimes were connected. James and Antoinette realised that both they, and the gallery, were once more in the spotlight. As much as they hated it, they knew it was unavoidable and they themselves were desperate to find out who murdered Constantin.

Chapter Sixteen

Daniel West was a young, enthusiastic and ambitious reporter at the *Guernsey Herald*. He had all the papers and reports about events at La Perle and had followed the story closely. He knew the police had been baffled by such a strange case, and that they had sought help from French and English police, particularly after realising Constantin Patras had been murdered, and Raphael subsequently had disappeared. Attending police press conferences, he found himself not only interested but wondering if he could do a little investigating of his own. He was no detective but he could, he felt sure, do a good job of sniffing out a story, and he was confident there was something in this story to be found out. In fact, there was something very odd about the whole thing and especially about the artist.

A background story telling some interesting facts about him might prove worthy of coverage, not just in the *Herald*, but possibly in the national papers too. It wasn't often the word 'scoop' was used in connection with the Guernsey press, but Daniel's enthusiasm told him there might well be a scoop here. Somewhat nervous, he approached his editor explaining the mystery surrounding Mr Harcourt-Smythe, along with suspicions of his possible complicity in the murder. Would his editor allow him to do some digging, he asked nervously. And yes, his editor would, all expenses paid.

On a high, he set off to find out what he could… but information was hard to find. Harcourt-Smythe was a very elusive and private person. Daniel could find no trace of an address in Highgate, London, his supposed home. His only success was at La Perle, where Antoinette was able to provide Daniel with his studio address.

"At least I think this is it. I only know it because I saw it on the sender's address on the packaging when his paintings arrived in Guernsey. Is there a particular reason you want to know?"

"Well, only in as much as that I've found it interesting as I've covered the various stories and reports in the Herald. He seems to be a bit of a mystery man, and I thought that if we knew more about him, it might help find him too."

"That's true," she agreed, "so good luck."

"Thank you."

As Daniel left for London, he felt he had very slim pickings and his task would not be so easy. Nevertheless, he was excited at the opportunity.

London proved mesmerising, exciting, but also disconcerting. At the back of his mind was the thought that he was on a wild-goose chase, and he felt increasingly anxious as well as far less confident. Settling into a hotel near Hyde Park, however, he realised what a great opportunity his editor had given him. He would not be deterred, and he relaxed and made his plans over dinner. 'I'll feel a real fool back in Guernsey if I don't find out anything, so I must not fail, and London does seem to be the place to begin my search.'

Next morning, full of optimism, he set off for Raphael's studio, which took longer to find than he thought, and it was a surprise when he did. The studio was in a part of London that, politely, could only be described as past its best. 'Why on earth would he have a studio here? In a building that's almost derelict? Surely I can't just knock on the door and expect Raphael to answer? That would be too ridiculously easy. Even so, there might be some clues if I can at least get in somehow.' He hesitantly rang the bell of what was a large, dilapidated Victorian house, now divided into flats. Daniel looked around nervously, feeling uncomfortable. To his surprise, the main door opened and a woman stood there; she wore an apron and her hair was covered in dust and cobwebs, but her smile was welcoming.

"Can I help you?"

"I'm looking for Mr Harcourt-Smythe. Am I at the right address?"

"You are, but he isn't here at the moment," she answered in a northern accent.

Daniel was deflated and didn't quite know what to do. The woman must have noticed his crestfallen demeanour.

"Why did you want to see him?" she asked, now a little wary. Daniel explained that he was a reporter and had come over from the Channel Islands. He briefly explained about the police's suspicions. When she saw his ID, she relaxed. She smiled again. "You'd better come in then. I'm his sister Tanya," she said, leading him into a small ground-floor flat. "Come in, take a seat." She gave him another warm smile. He liked her immediately. "Well, that is, take a seat if you can find one in all this mess." She wasn't wrong. The whole place was a shambles and looked as if it had been burglarised. But it was clearly Raphael's studio, evident by his easels, pictures stacked against the walls and paint splatters covering everything from walls to floors and furniture. They sat on two ancient upright chairs. "Yes, I know it's a mess," Tanya said before he could comment. "Raffy asked me if I'd clear out everything for him – I didn't think it would be in such a state. I've never been here before."

"Are you close to your brother, then?"

Tanya snorted. "Definitely not! I hadn't heard from him for ten years. He didn't want to know us when he became successful. He hid his background very well and didn't want to risk anyone finding out who he really was. Back then, he just thought he was too good for us. He rang me out of the blue. I don't even know how he had my number, and I only agreed because he offered me a lot of money. Well, it was a lot to me. Plus it gave me the chance to have a break in London in a nice hotel and everything. So I got on a train and here I am, but I have no idea where he is. He left the key under a stone; didn't think anyone did that anymore."

Daniel managed to get in a question while she took a breath. "So where did you get the train from?"

"Oh, from Durham, all our family are from there, I lived there for years."

"So, Raphael is from Durham too?"

"Course he is, just didn't like admitting it to anyone. He was always ashamed of his working-class roots."

"But he claimed he was from Highgate in London."

She laughed. "He does come from Highgate, but not in London. It's an old mining town in Durham."

Daniel's face must have registered his surprise. "No wonder I couldn't find an address for him here."

"Oh yes, he lied about a lot of things did our Raffy, even his name." Daniel was again surprised, but confident in his hunch that there was something not right about Raphael Harcourt-Smythe. "Listen, do you fancy a cup of tea?" asked Tanya. "It's nice to be able to talk about all this because I just didn't know what to do." She went to a makeshift kitchen in a corner.

"So what did you mean about his name?" Daniel asked as the kettle boiled.

"His real name is Ralph Smith, which was far too common for our Raff. He needed to make himself much posher than that!" Tanya carried over two mugs, Daniel noticing the big chips in them as she handed his over. "Don't worry, they're clean, I gave them a good scrub. The whole place needs a good scrub if you ask me."

Daniel nodded and smiled. He liked this open and down-to-earth woman. She knew he was a reporter but was happy, and possibly even relieved, to talk about her brother. "So where does he live, if not in Highgate in London?"

"He didn't tell me – he's always been secretive and thinking he was superior to everyone. Tell you what I think, though. I think he's been living here, at least for a while. If you were desperate, you could manage with the little kitchen and a pull-out bed, and there's a tiny bathroom."

"I suppose you could," agreed Daniel, "but what makes you think he's been living here?"

"I'm not one hundred percent sure, but for one thing, all his mail comes here. He's in trouble, our Raff. Here, I'll show you something." She picked up a pile of letters from the floor. "See! These bank statements keep arriving. Take a look."

Shocked, Daniel said "I can't look at these, they are confidential."

"Well, I have, though not at first. Like you, I thought it was none of my business. Then two days ago, not long after I'd arrived here, there was a knock at the door and guess what it was – bailiffs! I didn't let them in, told them I was the cleaner and said to come back when Raffy was here. I knew then something was really wrong. I was so angry with Raffy, involving me in his shady life but I shouldn't have been surprised really. He'd left me a mobile number, but it turned out to be a false one, so I couldn't speak to him. So, I thought I was justified in opening the mail. Honestly, I couldn't believe what I was seeing. There were loads of bills and when I came to the bank statements I had to sit down, I was so shocked. I couldn't believe the amount of money he owes, thousands and thousands. The final letter said he was to be taken to the bankruptcy court. To top it all, there were two official notes from the police; twice they seemed to have come to find him, asking him to contact them urgently. I daresay they are now attempting to get a warrant to get in here. I didn't know what to do about that either. I really should contact them, but I'm really scared to get too involved."

Daniel was equally shocked. This was not what he had expected, nor could he stop Tanya as everything came gushing out. "Then, this morning, this arrived," she said, holding up another letter. It's a claims form from an insurance company. I can't imagine what he's claiming for, but it just gets worse and worse."

But Daniel thought he did know and suddenly, quite a few things started to make sense, and if he was right, the insurance claim was for Madrigal. But what did that mean? He had much to think about.

"I don't know what to do with any of it." Tanya seemed overwhelmed. "I'm so sorry, I've just blurted all this out, but you are the first person I could talk to who seemed to have some involvement with what is going on. I'm so confused and still furious with Raffy, who has used me shamelessly. Just before you arrived, I'd decided I was going to go back home. I don't want anyone to think I'm involved. I suppose I should have known, Raffy has always been bad news. Now I'm not even sure if my hotel has been paid, probably not, and I don't expect the money he promised me will materialise either. What a mess!"

"One thing I'm very confused about," Daniel said, "is where has all his money gone? He prides himself on being rich and famous, and of how valuable his paintings are. How do you know he's telling the truth" He's a liar and a cheat, it seems to me." Then suddenly Daniel remembered about the scandal with the lifeboat donation and how Raphael's cheque had bounced and was never re-presented. Tanya could be right, and he decided to tell more of the events unfolding in Guernsey. "There's more to the story than I told you. Yes, one of his paintings was stolen from his exhibition at a

141

Guernsey gallery. Since then his agent, Constantin Patras, has been found murdered, and Raphael is the police's main suspect."

Tanya visibly paled and she almost fell from her upright chair.

"Oh, God, it's worse than I thought." Daniel gave her time to take it all in and recover her composure. She looked slowly around the studio. "When you look at this place, why would an artist worth millions have a place like this as a studio? It's grubby, a complete mess and everything is cheap or old. I think it says it all, don't you?"

"Yes, I'd have to agree."

"So should I just go home?"

"Probably, yes, Raphael can't expect you to clear up all his mess, but by the fact of what I've told you, you have a responsibility to tell the police."

"But I don't want to hang around here any longer, I want to go home."

"Well, what if you go back and speak to the police there? You could take all these bills and letters, and anything else you've found here that you think may be useful. The London police are obviously working with those in Guernsey. The Durham police can send everything to Guernsey."

"That sounds like a good plan. Thank you, that's what I'll do. I'll lock the door, tell the police and let them sort it out. Oh, I feel better now. I'm glad you came, Daniel." She gave him the happiest of smiles.

"So, when do you think you'll leave?"

"Probably tomorrow. There's a bit to do, not least finding the money to pay the hotel bill – it won't be cheap."

Daniel realised he didn't want Tanya to disappear out of his life so soon. 'What's wrong with me?' he said to himself. 'I've only just met her – I know nothing about her.' Yet he liked her. He admired her frank openness, her somewhat naive trust and her expressive blue eyes, now revealing the sadness she felt and her gullibility. He sensed, though, that she was a kind person, always ready to help people. Bravely, he took the initiative. "Tanya, I'm staying in London tonight too. Would you like to join me for dinner?"

Tanya's mouth dropped open slightly. "What? Why would you want to take me out for dinner?"

"Well, we've helped each other, and it would be company too. Better than eating alone. And, well, I like you!"

Tanya blushed and then thought about what Daniel had said. "Okay, that would be very nice, thank you."

Daniel felt quite light-hearted, realising he spoke the truth: he really did like her. With her hair washed and brushed and apron discarded, Tanya was transformed when they met for dinner in a small Italian restaurant close to Daniel's hotel. She looked less stressed and more relieved, knowing that she had made the decision to go home. The highlights in her dark brown hair shimmered in the lights and she had greeted him with her wide and friendly smile. Daniel again sensed a warm, caring and kind woman, and he responded to her warmth. They found conversation easy, Tanya asking about Guernsey and he about Durham, a place he knew a little about because an old school friend had been a student at the university there. Daniel said he was sorry about the sailing accident her father had experienced in Guernsey, and why Raphael said he wanted to reward the lifeboat service for his rescue.

While telling his tale, Tanya had a very confused look.

"Stop, Daniel. You mean my dad, Gerald Smith?"

"That's what he said."

Tanya shook her head. "It's another of his lies, isn't it? My father has never been to Guernsey so far as I know, and he has never so much as been on a yacht. He hates sailing."

They were both, once again, subdued. Where did Raphael's lies end and the real Raphael begin? It could well be a tangled web that could never be fully unravelled. Both enjoyed their meal, perhaps more than they thought they would, and Daniel insisted on accompanying her to the train station next morning. Tanya waved as she boarded the train, happy to be going home, but infinitely sad to have realised the evil which seemed to have settled on her brother. Daniel slipped a piece of paper into her hand with his contact details but she put it into her pocket without looking at it. As the train pulled out of the station, he shouted "It would be nice to see you again, Tanya! Give me a ring!" But would she? Only time would tell.

Chapter Seventeen

Whilst Daniel was away, there had been further developments back in Guernsey. Kathleen Groves was taken aback when she spotted the photo in her local post office. She knew straightaway that she recognised the man. For many years Kathleen had owned and run her little kiosk café adjacent to Ca'lou beach. As well as basic food and drink, she sold other things like beach toys and windbreakers. Most of her trade was take-away, but, in a little space to the side, she had a few tables and chairs, brightened up with pots of summer flowers. She had never made much money, but she loved what she did. It was a popular beach and she relished being close to the sea. Locals always stopped for a chat, and she met lots of friendly visitors too. There was always something to see and she enjoyed watching people walk out to the little Ca'lou island at low tide. Sometimes she would arrive at dawn, enjoying the solitude, watching the sun rise over the little island. Her only companions were seabirds; gulls squawking and terns swooping. Then there were the flocks of waders, dunlin, greenshank and brightly coloured but noisy oyster catchers arriving as the tide receded. The stars of the show were the little egrets, their plumage shimmering white in the early morning light; Mediterranean birds extending their territory, they were relative newcomers to the Channel Islands. Their numbers were growing year on year and visitors sought out these rare UK birds, which could also be seen on neighbouring islands.

It was because it was unusual to see anyone at sunrise that she remembered him. He wasn't alone that day. He was with another man and they landed on Ca'lou by boat, the owners of which she didn't recognise. There was no-one else on the island as far as she could see. With nothing much else to do, she watched as they made their way to the German bunker, and she wondered why on earth they would want to go there at this time of day. It wasn't a nice place at any time and it would be bitterly cold, an unnatural cold. After a while, but still very early, the sun now higher and promising a fine day, both men were landed on the beach and the boat quickly sped away. They approached the kiosk and asked for a 'much needed drink'. They were her only customers; she had had a really good look at them both and was therefore confident about identification. She wasted no time in contacting the police. Later, she remembered she had seen the man again on another day, but not so clearly this time as it was in the early morning mist which clung to the island, with the sun struggling to come through.

On the basis of Kathleen's sightings, the police planned a search. Surely Mr Smythe wasn't hiding out there? The bunker was a vile place and Janice couldn't imagine anyone staying there for any length of time. Nevertheless, it had been a reliable sighting.

Chapter Eighteen

Daniel had more investigations planned. Having looked on the internet, he had found a list of galleries in London where Raphael had exhibited, and decided to visit some to see what he could find out.

The Hyacinth Gallery in Kensington was his first success. As soon as he asked the owners if they knew Raphael, they became immediately agitated.

"What do you want to know?" a woman asked suspiciously.

"I believe he had an exhibition here and wondered if it was true?"

"Oh it's true, I'm sad to say. Lying little toad, he was."

"Stella darling," her partner said, "calm down and we'll see what this gentleman wants."

"I'm over from Guernsey," Daniel explained, "a reporter from the local paper and I'm investigating a potential fraud at one of his exhibitions in Guernsey."

"Then you've come to the right place." Stella seemed angry. "If, that is, you need clarification and confirmation that he is a cheat, a thief and a liar. I won't go into too much detail, but Raffy cheated us out of a lot of money when he held an exhibition here. I can guarantee that fraud and Raffy go perfectly well together. The gallery almost went under, but by some miracle we are still here. If you find him, strangle him for me."

"Thank you, you've been very helpful. Would it be OK to use the information you have given?"

"By all means – the man needs to be stopped."

* * *

Daniel had approached The Tate but understood when they refused to give an interview. While confirming that Raphael had had an exhibition there, they were reluctant to say anything more.

Daniel was not disheartened, however, as he had other places to go. The Templefield Gallery in Southwark was highly regarded, not quite as much as the Tate but its reputation was excellent. It was a large, popular gallery that attracted many of the best London artists. Daniel, however, still found it difficult to secure an appointment, but his persistence and the mention of Raphael's name was enough. One of the managers who had worked with Raphael's exhibition agreed to meet with him. His success, however, seemed short-lived.

"I'm sorry, Mr West, but apart from confirming that Mr Harcourt-Smythe did hold an exhibition here, I can't really divulge much more. It's a confidential matter, you see. I hope you understand." She got up to leave, intending for Daniel to do the same. As she walked off, he held back and said, "But this is about a murder; Mr Harcourt-Smythe is a murder suspect in Guernsey."

The manager stopped mid-step. "Are you serious?"

"Deadly serious. That's why I have come over from Guernsey so I can find out more about him."

That did the trick. The manager came back and sat down. "He defrauded us out of thousands of pounds," she said. "He also lied about sales, pretending – as we now realise – that some of his work had been sold for incredible amounts of money. He told us that they had been bought by anonymous buyers and he would handle the sales himself. We later discovered that they hadn't been sold at all, or where they had been sold, he defrauded us out of our commission."

"Why didn't you prosecute him?"

"Well, it was hard to prove and also," she admitted, "it was probably because of professional pride. Nor did we want to be humiliated and lose the respect of the public." She finished by adding that her personal opinion of him was that he was arrogant, which covered up his lies and deception, along with his dishonesty. Daniel promised not to mention the name of the gallery, but the facts would speak for themselves.

Chapter Nineteen

Back on Guernsey, the police were keen to follow up on the sightings at Ca'lou, so decided to undertake a thorough search of the bunker. Janice was glad of something positive to do and to be able to abandon her enquiries of the yacht owners, at least temporarily.

"I can't imagine Smythe hiding out here, can you?" asked the constable.

"No, I think it more likely he was visiting, but if so, we need to find out why."

"Not looking forward to this though," added the inspector. "It's pretty awful in there."

"You've been in before, have you sir?"

"Yes, I have. It's pitch black in most places, dirty and full of bat droppings."

"Oh, lovely," Janice commented drily.

"Exactly, but come on, let's get on with it."

It took only minutes at a brisk pace to walk across the causeway, where the bunker loomed up in front of them, the door slightly ajar. They had strong torches and stepped reluctantly inside. It was a known bat-roost and was protected as such by the local wildlife trust, but nevertheless the police were not prepared for the smell and sudden assault as hundreds of bats swarmed around their heads, disturbed by the intrusion. It was scary, like something from a movie. They stood still and the bats calmed down and returned to their roost in the dark corners.

"Oh, this is horrible," said Janice who did not relish going further into the bunker. The empty shell of the bunker was echoey and they found themselves whispering. Their torches threw eerie shadows, also highlighting the floor covered with years of debris, bat droppings and unknown other things they didn't really want to think about.

"There are lots of ashes and fire-remains here. Why is that?" asked the constable.

It was the inspector who answered, "Youngsters use it as a den and light fires to keep warm. Can't see the attraction myself and it's deathly cold in here."

Janice added, "I've heard they use it as a kind of dare, seeing how long they can stay in here."

"Yes, I've heard that. I bet they don't stay long."

"Too right, and nor do I," the constable said under his breath.

"There is a strange atmosphere in here; it's no wonder people say it's haunted." Janice shivered.

As they moved from room to room, they checked the fire remains and the rubbish strewn about the floor.

"What was he doing here? There doesn't seem to be anything to indicate…" and Janice's words were cut off as she was interrupted by Constable Swann.

"Over here, sarge, I think I've found something."

"Where are you?" The constable shone his torch to indicate where he was. They both joined him and found he was pointing to a partially burned large pile, which someone had evidently tried to cover up, unsuccessfully.

"It looks like a recent fire, different to the others." Dean picked up a piece of wood to poke among the remains. "What do you think?" he asked them.

"Don't know yet, but let's have a closer look." Janice shone her light on the embers.

"Hang on!" she exclaimed. "What did that painting look like? There seems to be bits of canvas here, and I think there are daubs of paint on a scrap of material." Suddenly, Janice was excited, feeling that they were getting somewhere. "What do you think, Inspector?"

"It's certainly possible. I didn't see any pictures of the painting. Do either of you know what it looks like?"

"Sergeant Fontaine and I both got a description, sir," Constable Swann replied.

"Tell us then," said the inspector urgently.

"Well, according to the gallery owners, it wasn't a conventional painting, but it was huge. Apparently, a massive canvas and silk work that hung down in the room from the gallery ceiling. It didn't have a frame. It was apparently vibrant too, lots of deep reds, blues and purples."

The inspector looked at him, surprised. "Well done, constable. Maybe, then, we have found it; if it was so big it would have taken ages to burn, leaving remnants like this."

"Thank you, sir." The constable, proud but embarrassed too, wandered slightly away and approached the lighter area of the bunker where the open gun emplacement and watch tower was situated and where he continued to scour the ground. They heard him shout.

"Inspector! Sergeant! Over here!" When they joined him he pointed to a dark smudge on the ground, more clearly visible because of the light seeping in from the large opening.

"What is it, constable?"

"Here sarge, it looks like blood."

Looking closely at the smudge, they had to agree, and all three continued their search for further evidence. And there was.

"Here!" shouted the inspector, who was by the lookout. He pointed to the shelf where there was more blood. Finally, it seemed their search had been worth it.

"OK, let's get out of here. Get the door sealed and bring down the forensics. And, Constable Swann," the inspector continued, "we need you to stay here until they arrive, and don't let anyone else in. This is now a potential crime scene."

"Will do, sir." Constable Swann was none too happy about being left alone in such a spooky place. Fortunately, he was able to stay outside and sit on the rough grass looking over to the mainland.

* * *

"So, what do we think, Sergeant?" the inspector addressing her as they drove back to police HQ in St Peter Port.

"I think two scenarios, sir. One is that Patras stole the paining and tried to get rid of it by burning it. Harcourt-Smythe found him and killed him, whether deliberately or not, I don't know.

"What would his motive have been to steal it, Sergeant?"

"Patras and Smythe had argued, resulting in Patras being sacked. It could simply have been revenge."

The inspector continued questioning. "So what about scenario two?"

"Smythe could have stolen the painting, Patras found out and Smythe killed him." "But what was Smythe's motive?" the inspector countered, "Why would he steal his own painting and destroy it? It doesn't make sense. Yet even the motive of Patras seems a stretch."

"I know it does, sir."

"One thing we do know is that it was Patras who died. The questions remain. Who stole the painting and why? Why destroy it? Who killed Patras? and where is Smythe?"

Both had much to think about and nothing seemed straightforward.

Chapter Twenty

After his contacts with the London galleries, Daniel tried to piece together what he had learned. His crossing back to Guernsey was a rough one. There was a heavy swell and the ferry was pitching and rolling. But he hardly noticed; he was elated and sat outside, remembering what he had done using his initiative, his method of investigation giving him a lot of information. It was a professional satisfaction that was rarely possible in Guernsey. When he arrived back and approached his editor's office, he was literally grinning from ear to ear.

"Daniel, I take it the trip was worthwhile then. How was the sail?"

"It was rough sailing back but it didn't matter, it was really worth the journey."

"Just as well then, Dan, after the expenses you've charged us." However, his editor was laughing and Daniel knew after he told him of his findings that he had done well, and his editor was impressed.

"You'll need to go straight to the police with the information you know, Daniel – it's crucial evidence. Then after that, we can run it in the paper."

"Under my by-line, sir."

"Of course, Daniel, this is your work, you've done well."

"Thank you, sir. Shall I go to the police straight away then?"

"Might as well. Stress to them, though, that as we've have helped them, we expect a heads-up on the story when it's solved."

Daniel had a spring in his step as he left for the police station.

* * *

The police had made considerable headway but were still puzzled by the who and why, especially in respect of the motive.

"There's another element here that we just don't seem to be getting," Fontaine told her inspector. "And we are assuming that Smythe was in the bunker and that Patras was murdered there."

"You're right, we need the results from forensics. We don't even know if the two of them were there together. Ms Groves identified Smythe, but not Patras. It could have been another person altogether, and we've no idea who that might be," Janice concurred. "They might just have been visiting and with nothing sinister about it."

"Unlikely, though. We need to wait for the test results and see what they tell us," concluded the inspector.

Outside the inspector's office, Janice was feeling frustrated and annoyed with herself. Even though the case was not clear-cut, she felt she had not impressed Inspector Louvaine, and that, despite her efforts, she had been found wanting. But there were too many scenarios, and she wondered if, perhaps, Smythe was dead too. She needed more concrete evidence as to what was going on here.

Later that day, the forensic results came in, quicker than she had hoped.

"So, the scraps were part of the painting," she said.

"Yes, we confirmed that after showing them to the gallery owners."

"And the blood?" Janice held her breath, hoping it would prove to be that of Patras.

"The blood is a perfect match for Constantin Patras. He had an unusual blood group, AB, so there isn't any doubt about it."

"What about other blood traces on the bunker shelf?"

"Unless there are any blood traces we haven't found, which is very unlikely, we are confident the only blood was that of Mr Patras."

"Thank you for getting the results so quickly."

Janice gave a sigh of relief that her belief that Mr Patras was killed in the bunker had been vindicated. Yet, she found she wasn't much further forward; she still had so much to do.

* * *

Next morning, a thoughtful and somewhat disconsolate sergeant was in her office and brooding over a cup of coffee. She jumped when her phone rang.

"There's a gentleman to see you, Sergeant," the station receptionist said.

"Do you know who it is?"

"Actually, it's Mr West from The Herald."

"Oh no, not a reporter, I just don't think I can cope with him now. What does he want anyway?"

"He says he has some urgent news for you; he's quite adamant. I think you should see him."

Janice hesitated, then said "OK, send him up." She hoped she could soon get rid of him. There was a quiet knock and she opened the door to see a young man, obviously excited, and with a captivating smile. She had met him before but didn't really know him.

"I know you must be busy, but I have some important information about Mr Harcourt-Smythe."

"You do? Then come in, Mr West and take a seat."

"Thank you."

"I take it you've seen or spoken to him?"

"No, I'm afraid not." Janice's hopes sank. Daniel must have seen her expression. "But listen, I have some vital information."

"Go on then, Mr West, I'm listening," she said but her voice showed little enthusiasm.

He sensed she wasn't really interested but continued anyway. "You see," began Daniel, "Mr Harcourt-Smythe is not who he seems. My editor gave me permission to go to London to try and find out what I could about him." Janice's ears suddenly pricked up and she was eager to hear what Mr West had to say. She sat on the edge of her seat.

"Okay, carry on."

He told her of the false name, how he contrived to create a persona for himself, so that people believed he was a famous, wealthy artist. He managed then to find his way into the most prestigious galleries. "However, he is a liar, a fraud and a cheat. The galleries I contacted said he had cheated them out of lots of money, some barely managing to survive. In some cases he said he had sold paintings for large sums of money and didn't pay the commission. And there is a lot more I found out."

"Carry on then, but apart from the galleries, where did you get the information?"

"From his studio."

"But, Mr West, how could you? The police in London tried at least twice to access his studio but couldn't. No-one was there, and no-one had seen him. I believe they are hoping to get a warrant to get in."

"I think they must have tried there before me. When I arrived, his sister was there. Mr Harcourt-Smythe had contacted her and asked if she would clear the studio for him. It was his sister who was able to give me more information about her brother. His real name is Ralph Smith and he comes from Highgate in County Durham, not Highgate, London. Among the other important things she told me was the fact that he owed thousands of pounds to the banks and other individuals. He was about to be declared bankrupt. Even the bailiffs arrived when she was there. He never contacted her in London and he just landed her with all these problems."

Sergeant Fontaine was dumbstruck. "Well, what a wonderful job you've done. Thank you. Do you think it would be possible to speak to this sister?"

"Well, she's actually gone back home. She didn't want to get involved when she realised the mess her brother had put her in. She took all the correspondence with her and was going to give it to the police, as well as to make a statement. I imagine the mainland police are intending to send all the documentation over to you."

"I can check on that. Where would she have gone, do you think?"

"Probably her own police station in Highgate, but it could have also been passed on to the county police in Durham."

"Thank you so much, Daniel." Once again she received his lovely smile.

"So, what shall I do now?"

"Could you put down in writing everything you've found, anything you think relevant, and send it here to me? As soon as we've assimilated everything, I'll get back to you. You've done a good job, you should be proud."

"I'll do it straight away. But, just one thing – my editor says that as we have helped with the investigation, could we please be given priority on the story?" Daniel looked at her earnestly.

She smiled. "How could I say no?"

"Thank you." He virtually leapt off his chair and headed to the door, giving Janice another of his dazzling smiles.

"Oh, I've just remembered one thing," Daniel said as he popped his head back round the door. "The last letter Tanya, his sister, said arrived was from an insurance company, a claim form for theft."

"Was it now?" and the information gave Janice more to contemplate. 'That's a nice young man,' she said to herself after the door closed, then immediately checked herself. 'Good grief! I must be getting old' and she laughed at herself.

* * *

Shortly after Daniel had left, Janice's phone rang again. It was Inspector Louvaine. "Could you come up to my office, Janice?"

"Certainly, sir. In fact I was just about to ring you. I have some more information." Janice joined the inspector in his office where the information was exchanged.

"I've just had a call from the police chief at Durham. Perhaps you know something?"

"I do, sir."

"OK. Well, apparently a young woman by the name of Tanya Smith attended the police station saying she had information about a possible crime. When interviewed she made a statement saying she was the sister of Harcourt-Smythe and also had documents and letters relevant to him."

"This was what I was going to talk to you about." She proceeded to relay all the information that Daniel had told her.

"This sister has gone back home now, but do we want to go over there and interview her ourselves?"

"What did they say about the quality of the statement?"

"Apparently, it was long, thorough and compelling. They also said that all the documents have been lodged with them and asked what we wanted them to do with them."

"May I suggest, sir, that for now they can send a transcript of Tanya's statement and letters here and, if we think it inadequate, then we can arrange to interview her."

"That sounds sensible and it will hopefully save us a journey to Durham."

They waited for all the information to arrive and were impressed at the depth and quality of detail. They saw no need to see Tanya Smith again, but a letter thanking for her co-operation would be sent.

While waiting for the information to arrive, Janice repeatedly went over all the possible scenarios in her head, as well as making innumerable jottings. Then, for some reason, she thought back to her interview with Eleanor Grant. She remembered how upset she had been and how reluctant she was to disclose something which Patras had told her in confidence.

"What was it she said?" Janice cast her mind back. Then it came to her. Mr Patras mentioned to Ms Grant that Smythe had been very drunk and, in a careless moment, he divulged to his agent a secret which he never intended anyone to know. On sobering up, Raphael realised what had done and he told his agent he must not tell anyone. But Mr Patras had been appalled and distressed by what he had heard and wondered what he ought to do with this information. As far as the sergeant knew, this secret stayed with Mr Patras. Did he die because of it? What was it Mr Patras knew? A secret that, if revealed, could devastate Smythe. Did he eventually feel compelled to kill Mr Patras because it was too dangerous for him to know about it? Thoughts tumbled through her mind, all the things she had heard in her investigations and what it told her about Harcourt-Smythe. The secret, the studio, the sister, the theft, the letters, the debts, the fraud, the insurance. Suddenly, she knew, and she dashed out urgently to speak to the inspector. Now she was certain about what happened at La Perle gallery on the night of their exhibition opening. The sequence of events seemed perfectly clear in her mind.

Chapter Twenty-One

The inspector and sergeant now realised they needed to step up their manhunt in earnest. They also felt an obligation to meet with the people who had been both involved and affected by the theft and subsequent murder. It was possible, they hoped, that some more information might come to light.

So, Antoinette, James, Eleanor and Daniel met with the police at La Perle. They were all expectant of finding out about the crime, but they were despondent too after all that had happened. They looked at each other apprehensively, but with anticipation. Eleanor seemed very quiet, but more composed and not quite as pale as previously. Antoinette and James just wanted an end to it all, whilst Daniel was energised, pleased at being asked to attend.

"You are probably wondering why we have asked to meet with you here," Inspector Louvain began. No-one answered, but all four looked at him. "Well, the reason is that Mr Harcourt-Smythe is both a murderer and a cheat," he said, at which there was a sharp intake of breath. "There are still some details to be worked out, but we believe that Smythe stole his own painting and murdered Mr Patras."

There was a gasp from Eleanor. Antoinette stared at the Inspector in disbelief and James went pale.

"But that doesn't make any sense, Inspector. Why would he steal his own painting?" Antoinette said, astonished.

"I'll explain all, and then, hopefully, you'll understand."

"OK," replied Antoinette, and all of them settled more comfortably, sensing a long story.

Eleanor had arranged the café informally for the meeting, so there were comfortable sofas and low coffee tables, creating a more reassuring and less threatening atmosphere. They sipped hot drinks, trying to relax.

"It's hard to know where to begin," continued the inspector, "but first let me say that Mr Harcourt-Smythe is not his real name. We have Mr Daniel West to thank for his assistance in gathering information, and that is why the reporter is here today."

"So, who is he really then?" James asked.

"His real name is Ralph Smith. He does not live in Highgate in London, but rather comes from a former coal mining village in Durham called Highgate. Having found out all this, and more, I can tell you that the whole plan for Mr Smith and the exhibition has been a fraud from the outset, a hoax and deliberate deception of those involved."

Antoinette felt faint; she looked at James who took her hand. He, too, was shocked.

"What do you mean, a set up?" asked James quietly.

"I'm trying not to be too long-winded, Mr Kerrissey. I know what a great shock it is to you all, so I'll try to clarify. It seems that Smith has lied for years. He did not earn millions of pounds from his paintings. In fact, he pretended they were sold when they weren't. He cheated gallery owners out of thousands of pounds."

Antoinette was finding it hard to listen and wanted some fresh air but knew she would have to stay and listen to it all. She let her head rest on the back of the sofa and closed her eyes. Sergeant Fontaine saw her distress and went to get her a glass of water.

"His life caught up with him, however, and earlier this year action was taken to declare him bankrupt. So what was he to do? He decided he could set up a great scam. Why not hold an exhibition here on Guernsey? No-one here would have had contact with him and no-one would question his success and wealth. What a good excuse, too, to pretend his father had been rescued by the lifeboat as his basis for choosing Guernsey."

"So that was a lie too," James said, becoming angry.

"Oh yes, his sister confirmed to Daniel that his father had never been to Guernsey. Apparently Ralph didn't even care for his father and hadn't seen him for over ten years."

"This gets worse," whispered Antoinette.

"I'm afraid it does, Ms Duchenne," he continued. "So, he thinks why not make a fuss of a special exhibit and make sure it has excessive insurance of ten million pounds. Then, when he steals the painting he makes a claim from the insurance company for it. He knew it hadn't been sold, but he had put a red dot on it and fooled everyone."

"It makes us seem so gullible, so foolish, it's quite embarrassing." Antoinette found herself ashamed, remembering how she had initially fallen for his charms; it was all pretence. "Oh James," she said. "I'm so sorry."

"No," continued the inspector, "not foolish, or stupid. He was a desperate man and he was clever. Too clever in the end."

"So, he must have stolen the painting the night of the exhibition. He must have come back and of course he knew how to switch off the alarm," James realised.

"Then, having found the bunker and its reputation, that it was infrequently visited, it must have seemed a perfect hiding spot." Sergeant Fontaine, who had taken up the story continued. "Then he would need to dispose of it properly. What he hadn't taken into account was Mr Patras, his honest agent, who Smith was quite happy to have take the blame later. It was you, Ms Grant, who gave us the clue." Eleanor quickly lifted her head to look at the sergeant.

"Me?" she asked, confused. "How did I help you?"

"Do you remember, Eleanor, how you were uncomfortable when telling us that Constantin had been told a secret?"

"I do, but how was that important?"

"When Smith was drunk," explained Fontaine, "he told Mr Patras a secret he should never have revealed. You told us, Eleanor, that Mr Patras was absolutely shocked by what he'd heard. Then when Smith sobered up, he realised what he'd done and tried to get Patras out of the way by sacking him, hoping that he would leave Guernsey. But Patras was a good man, as you knew, Eleanor, and he wasn't that easy to get rid of."

Eleanor could no longer hold back the tears, grieving that Constantin had been murdered.

"What Smith told Mr Patras, we believe, was that he had stolen Madrigal and hidden it, and furthermore, he was going to claim for its insured price of ten million. Not only that, but he presumably did not care how this affected La Perle and its owners. He was probably derisive and, as we know, he cared for no-one but himself. We can only surmise how angry Mr Patras was, but we believe he kept a close watch on Smith's movements and discovered him hanging around the bunker. At some point Mr Patras confronted him and Smith murdered him. With great difficulty, I imagine, he disposed of Mr Patras' body by throwing it into the sea from the gun emplacement. He didn't drown, by the way – he was dead before he entered the water. Then, as we know, his battered body was washed up on the shore several days later."

Eleanor couldn't take any more, running from the room in tears. Antoinette followed her to try and comfort her in her grief.

"And still we haven't found this evil man!" shouted James.

"No, but by God we will!" the inspector shouted back. As the police finished their testimony, they left behind a subdued group of people who could barely believe what they had been told.

"Please remember that what we have told you is in the strictest confidence; you will tell no-one anything at this vital stage of the investigation."

The police left in a hurry in order to issue another bulletin. The witnesses left behind at La Perle were stunned and bewildered by what they had been told, but were grateful that the police had done so, otherwise the police bulletin would indeed have created deep shock.

Police Bulletin

Guernsey police is urgently requesting the help of the public in finding Mr Raphael Harcourt-Smythe, also known as Mr Ralph Smith, who is wanted for murder, fraud and theft. Formerly staying on the island, it is believed that he has now left, probably by private boat or yacht, and his whereabouts are unknown. His description was released previously. If you think you have seen this man, or know his location, then please tell the police immediately. A special telephone line has been established and free calls can be made at all times.

Searches were being undertaken throughout the Channel Islands and police on the UK mainland and France had also been alerted. Photographs of Smith were more widely distributed. London police were searching his studio for clues, but if he had another residence in London they were unable to identify it. For such extended searches, both the inspector and sergeant were much more confident that someone would spot Smith and that he would be arrested.

Chapter Twenty-Two

Guernsey was still warm, but the days were inevitably shortening, the intensity of light was changing and autumn was definitely in the air. At any other time, Antoinette would have enjoyed the beautiful autumn days, seeing the hedgerows on the green lanes changing colour, the leaves falling, allowing a clearer view down to the beaches and across the bays. However, it seemed almost impossible to dream that there would be better and brighter days ahead. The gallery was still officially closed and they had no idea when their lives would return to a semblance of normality, if they ever did. The confidential nature of the meeting with the police, and the knowledge gained from it, weighed heavily on them. Having to keep what they knew to themselves meant not being able to update family and friends. Negative thoughts were uppermost in James' and Antoinette's minds, and carrying on with any normal activities was simply impossible until Smith was apprehended. For her part, Antoinette was sure he was nowhere in the Channel Islands, and, in fact, no longer looked for him when she was out and about. At the same time her mind was obsessed with her memories of the last few months. 'How could she have been such a fool? Why couldn't she have seen through his façade? Was she really so naïve?' All these questions, and more, she asked herself over and over. 'He has used me shamelessly,' she told herself and she felt dirty and hurt. Then there was James. 'How could I have been so blind?' She knew now that he had loved her for years. 'Why didn't I notice?' Yes, she had been excited and completely absorbed with the new gallery, but she knew too that this was just an excuse. 'How could I not have realised that I was in love with him too? Surely I ought to have known why he invested in the gallery. Yes, he is a caring, generous and altruistic man, but what an idiot I've been!'

she told herself. 'And I hurt him so much. I let Raphael treat him like dirt, try to emasculate him, be condescending and rude. And had she been any better?' She could only shake her head. She was so ashamed.

'James, I am so sorry,' she said to herself, knowing she needed to tell him so to his face. 'How lucky I am. James could have been so disgusted with me, past caring. Yet despite everything he has remained by my side when I needed him. And suddenly, quite suddenly, on the opening night, I knew I loved him and always had. Perhaps this is the one good thing that's come out of all this mess, though I scarcely have the right to find true happiness, coming as it has from the tragedy of Constantin losing his own life by trying to do the right thing. Yes, he sacrificed his life to right the wrong he saw in Raphael's actions.' Antoinette's feelings were bitter-sweet, knowing she had to make some good from all this. 'James and I will have our lives together. Thank you, Constantin, you were a lovely, good and kind man.'

* * *

James was having different thoughts. He was thinking about his family. He knew his parents were ready to go home, but they were reluctant to do so until Raphael was found.

"You don't need to wait," James reassured them. "You know I'll keep you informed of everything. There is nothing else you can do. Go home and spend some time with Georgia. She's worried about you too. When I spoke to her, she said it would be good for you to be able to see Luca and her. Worrying isn't doing you any good, and I agree that I've seen little enough of my sister and Luca, but you can. Your staying here won't make finding Raphael any easier, unless he's staying at the Meribel."

"Oh James, don't," pleaded his mother. "Don't even think that that evil man could be here. The very thought makes me go cold. But James, we don't like leaving you, sweetheart, it's such a terrible time for you and it isn't over yet."

"I'm a big boy now mum," he said and Julia smiled. "Seriously, I will be alright, you know I will, and Antoinette and I will see it through together. You know, in a funny sort of way, our love for each other has blossomed because of this tragedy. Whatever happens, we'll be alright."

"OK then, if you're sure, we'll go home," answered Julia. "And, Johnny, it will mean you won't need to cancel your hospital appointment. And yes, we'll be able to spend time with Georgia and Luca for her birthday."

"I'll book the ferry for you both and come and see you off."

"Thank you, we'd like that."

* * *

Like all police bulletins, it was a case of wait and see, although Sergeant Fontaine found waiting hard. What was worse was that it seemed after a few days that no-one knew where Smith was, nor had anybody apparently seen him. The few calls the police had received came from people who, despite their sincerity, were mistaken, even though every supposed sighting had been followed up.

'He could be absolutely anywhere,' Janice told herself angrily. 'Why should he in the Channel Islands? Or even in France for that matter? He has no connection with this area. He probably made his escape ages ago and is miles away by now.'

Disconsolate, she nevertheless decided to wait for a few more days to see if there were any more calls. After all, there wasn't much else she could do. Police in England and France were still on alert, especially in London. At the same time the ferries and airport staff were being extra vigilant. Despite such measures, Janice believed he had escaped by yacht or fishing boat and Inspector Louvaine concurred with her thoughts, which led to visits to the various yacht clubs across the Channel Islands, where members and visitors had been questioned. It had all been to no avail and now the trail was cold, very cold. When Constable Swann met with his sergeant, he recognised her stern and subdued looks. He didn't need to ask if there had been any developments. "Is there anything I can do?" he asked her.

"Such as what?" she snapped.

"I don't know. I was just offering to help."

"Well, there isn't anything. I'll call you straightaway when I need you," she answered, more fiercely than he had ever known her to be before.

"Right." He left hastily, glad to be out of the way.

* * *

It was late in the day when Inspector Louvaine approached Janice in her office. "It's late, Sergeant – why don't you get on home? You can't do any more here today."

"But what if there's a call, sir?"

"Janice, those officers staffing the lines know to inform us straightaway if anything useful comes through, you know that."

"Yes, sir." Then she hesitated. "Alright, sir, I'll go home and see you in the morning. But you will let me know, won't you, sir?"

"Just go Janice, and goodnight!"

After she left, he went wearily back to his own office. He wouldn't go home; he wanted to wait for any overnight developments.

* * *

Next morning, there was an unexpected turn of events and Janice was glad she had come into work very early. She rushed up to the inspector's office.

"Sir," she said excitedly, "there's been a call, I've just come off the phone." She noticed the inspector was tired and drawn, his eyes red and his face pale. "Are you alright, sir?"

"I'm fine, Sergeant. Now tell me, this call sounds promising, does it?"

"Oh yes, very much so. It came in from France. I don't know all the details yet but the call was from a couple staying on their yacht at Honfleur in Normandy. They say they have seen Smith."

"Right, let's get on then. What are we waiting for?" He picked up his jacket and phone at the same time. "Have you any more details at all on the couple at Honfleur?" He listened, and then spoke again, "OK, arrange the police launch, and as soon possible, we'll meet you at the port. Come on, Sergeant, we're on our way to Honfleur."

"It's convincing then is it, sir?"

"It seems to be, but we need to find out more for sure. It seems this couple live on Guernsey and are just having a few days' holiday in Normandy on their yacht Burgundy Belle. Apparently, they were at the opening at La Perle and saw Smith there. They are convinced he's in Honfleur and know where he's staying."

They were at the port in a matter of minutes, and it seemed only seconds before the boat was launched and they were on their way. It was a speedboat, and they were confident of reaching Honfleur quickly, where the Guernsey couple and the Normandy police were waiting for them.

"Is this the break we're looking for, sir?" asked Janice as she was thrown back in her seat as the boat set off.

"I certainly hope so, I really do."

The sergeant, with flushed cheeks as the spray and wind whipped her skin, couldn't hide the smile on her face, excited at the thought she may finally solve the crime.

Chapter Twenty-Three

In the event, the next day's ferry was full, and so Julia and Johnny were in Guernsey for another day, which meant there was much less of a rush to pack. She began after breakfast, encouraging Johnny to take a stroll along the port and marina. She seemed to have endless presents for Luca and for Georgia, but she would have to squash them in somehow. Her phone rang. It was Alex.

"Julia, it's Alex. I heard you're off home?"

"Yes, James persuaded us – we're on the early ferry tomorrow."

"You can't go without saying goodbye. We've all had a terrible time of it, so Charles and I wondered if you would like to come for a meal tonight?"

"That would be lovely, Alex, but please let us take you out for dinner. We'll book a restaurant. James says Florian's is a good place – what do you think?"

"Florian's would suit us fine, it's lovely there. Thank you, that's really kind."

"That's great then, it will be so good to see you before we leave. Shall we say 7.30?"

As Julia put the phone down, Johnny returned.

"Hey, Julia," he said excitedly. "I've just been down by the marina and the police launch was there. Then I saw some officers get aboard in something of a hurry and it shot off like a bullet. They aren't half quick, those speedboats. Do you suppose it has anything to do with the La Perle business?"

"I don't know, let's hope it is. I wish everything was settled; I don't like leaving James like this."

"I know but James is right, we are just hanging around now worrying, and it isn't doing you or me any good."

"You're right," she admitted.

"Come here." Johnny went to Julia and gave her a big hug. "James will let us know what's happening and things will sort themselves out, won't they?"

"I suppose." Julia wiped away a tear.

"Now none of that, Jules – come on, look on the bright side. This horrible thing has brought James and Antoinette together, not just as partners at La Perle but as a couple and what could be better than that?"

Julia smiled at him: he was right of course. "Oh, by the way, Alex rang while you were out. We've arranged to go out for a meal tonight before we go home."

"That's a lovely idea. Now come on, let me help you with that packing."

* * *

Florian's was busy. Julia only just managed to book a table. She remembered James telling her how popular it was. It was a chilly night and no-one was eating out on the balcony, despite the lovely twinkly lights shining in the night and giving a romantic feel. Inside, it was comfortable and, although full, it wasn't too noisy. There was a good atmosphere and it helped Julia and Johnny to relax. They saw Charles and Alex arrive and waved them over to their table. They were pleased to see each other and realised it had been a good idea to meet before they left for home.

"Chilly tonight," said Alex, acknowledging the pleasant warmth of the restaurant, as she took off her wrap and put on the back of her chair.

"Have you seen the menu yet?" asked Charles.

"No," Johnny confirmed, "We've only just got here ourselves."

The waiter noticed them and quickly came over with a menu and extensive wine list. It was agreed that Johnny would choose the wine, deciding on a crisp Chardonnay and a rich and mellow claret. Choosing the food was hard, the menu containing a long and tempting list of dishes.

"We're sorry you're going – it's been lovely to share your company, even though it has turned out rather tragically. It's been pretty terrible, hasn't it?" whispered Alex.

Julia replied, "Yes, awful really, and I don't like leaving James, though he assures me he'll be fine, and I know he will, but still…"

"He won't be on his own, Julia – we'll look after him. But when all this is sorted out you must come back and have a proper break. Charles wondered if you would both like a few days with us on our boat. We could sail over to France, maybe?"

"And Johnny and I can do a bit more fishing, catch our own dinner perhaps?" suggested Charles.

"We would love that, wouldn't we Johnny? Thank you. We'll see you in better times."

The meals arrived and the conversation lapsed for a while as they enjoyed their food and wine.

"This is a fine claret, Johnny. What do you think?"

Johnny was about to speak when Alex's phone rang.

"It's Antoinette," Alex said. "Shall I take it?"

"Yes, yes, don't worry."

"Hi, darling, is everything OK? We're at Florian's with Julia and Johnny. They're leaving to go back to Gloucester tomorrow."

"Listen mum," Antoinette said. "We've heard on the grapevine that there's been a sighting of Raphael."

"Really? Where?"

"Not sure, but it seems someone rang the police claiming to know where he is. Then someone else told us they had seen the police launch shoot off at great speed, heading out to sea. Oh Mum, let's hope it's true – I want an end to this."

"I know, sweetheart, I hope it's true too. Listen, do you want to come over? Are you on your own?"

"No, actually I'm at James', so I'll be fine. We just wanted to let you know. Anyway, I'll speak to you tomorrow – and wish Johnny and Julia a calm sail home."

"Will do, darling, take care and love to James." Seeing the worry on Julia's face, she said quickly, "Everything is fine. She rang to say there is a rumour that someone has seen Raphael and the police are on his trail in the launch."

"That's what I saw earlier then," commented Johnny. "I told Julia I'd seen the police heading out across the harbour in a speedboat."

"That must be right then, but Antoinette doesn't know where they were heading."

"Whatever it is, it looks like there has been some development at last. Please let it be true, Alex," Julia said in a voice full of emotion.

They had finished and enjoyed their meal, but were restless and anxious, not knowing whether to be pleased about the rumour, or downcast if it proved to be a false lead.

* * *

The police launch wasted no time getting to Honfleur. It virtually flew over the bumpy waves. It was uncomfortable, but no-one complained. Normandy police, along with the Guernsey couple, were already waiting by the harbourside. Mooring up, the Guernsey police soon found Mr and Mrs Beauvaise, who stood by their yacht with two French policemen close by.

Inspector Louvaine shook the couple's hands and thanked the police officers for their time. Then he addressed the couple. "We really appreciate this," he said. "Is there somewhere we can go to talk?"

They settled for a quiet harbourside café.

"So," began the inspector, "what makes you think it was Mr Smythe?"

"Because we've seen him before," replied Mrs Beauvaise. "We attended the opening of the exhibition at La Perle and met him there. He was distinctive in his dress, so he was noticeable, but we spoke to him as well. We found him rather ingratiating."

"After that evening," continued her husband, "we decided, after a few days, to take our yacht and have some time away."

His wife took over, both being excitable and wanting and rushing to tell their story.

"We hadn't any real plans, but eventually we ended up here in Honfleur, which is a lovely little town. We sleep on our yacht but usually eat in one of the local restaurants."

"Is that where you saw him?" questioned Janice.

"Yes," the husband answered. "Last night we were eating at the Hotel Chambord, where there's a nice, covered terrace, so it is comfortable and warm. While waiting for our meal to arrive we watched a man, who was clearly very drunk, as he stumbled from table to table, finally making his way into the hotel proper."

"He actually passed our table," his wife said, "and we immediately recognised him. We'd seen his photo in Guernsey and had met him, of course, so we were sure it was him."

"So what did you do?" the inspector queried.

"To be honest, we weren't sure what to do. We didn't know whether he was still wanted, but then we decided to ring you this morning."

"Did you not think to ring last night?" the sergeant said, somewhat fiercely.

"Sorry but no, we didn't think; it seemed so late."

"You do know we may now have lost him. He may well have checked out."

"Alright, Sergeant, Mr and Mrs Beauvaise have done their best."

"Yes, sorry," she said.

"So shall we go over there now?" the inspector asked.

Everyone set off for the hotel at a rapid pace.

"Do you want us to come too," asked the couple.

"Yes, please do."

The hotel stood proudly on the harbourside promenade, an old 18th century characterful hotel; small but exclusive. Like many other buildings in the town and along the harbour, the outside walls were painted, making it bright and welcoming in primrose yellow with baskets and tubs holding a profusion of flowers.

The inspector approached the hotel reception, introducing both himself and the sergeant. His French wasn't great, but adequate, and the Honfleur police were there to help.

"Do you have a resident by the name of Raphael Harcourt-Smythe?"

"Let me check sir. I have only just arrived for my duty," said the receptionist. "Is he an Englishman, inspector?"

"He is. Why do you ask?"

"We have no-one by the name you mentioned, and only one gentleman from England."

"He may have used another name," interrupted Janice quickly. "It could be the name Gerald Durham, or Gerald Smith, or Ralph Smith."

"This gentleman is called that, Monsieur Gerald Durham."

"That's him sir. He comes from Durham, and his father is called Gerald." They all looked astounded, but she was right.

"Then could you show us to his room?"

"Oh, he isn't in his room, ma'am. You'll find him in the bar. I think he drinks quite a lot."

Without more ado, all the policemen rushed into the bar, just off the reception, and immediately spotted him in a corner, deep in thought.

The inspector looked quickly at the sergeant and Mr and Mrs Beauveise, and all nodded. Inspector Louvaine went straight up to him.

"Mr Ralph Smith, I am arresting you for the murder of Mr Constantin Patras, and also for theft and insurance fraud."

Obviously drunk, Smith soon recovered some composure. "Don't be ridiculous! Who do you think you are addressing?" he smiled smugly, while swaying slightly. "You have the wrong person. Who is this Ralph Smith? I've never heard of him. Now go away and leave me alone," he slurred.

"Perhaps then, we'll arrest you as Raphael Harcourt-Smythe, or Gerald Durham. Whatever you choose." Smith's mouth dropped open. "We are arresting you, sir." The inspector nodded to the police officers who grabbed him before he tried to run.

"Get off me! How dare you accost me! I'll sue you for this." Smith squirmed out of their hands and in his drunkenness stumbled and fell to the floor. The police picked him up and put on handcuffs. Then, suddenly, the fight seemed to go out of him; he slumped as he was led and half carried away to the police launch and back to Guernsey.

Janice and her inspector exchanged satisfied looks and smiled. They followed Smith out, back to the harbour. The couple who had identified him were equally pleased. Janice approached them and thanked them profusely. They would be proud of outing a murderer and they would certainly have a tale to tell. They walked back to their yacht, both with self-satisfied smiles, but their smiles could not have been wider than those of Inspector Louvaine and his sergeant.

Chapter Twenty Four

Whilst hiding away at his hotel, and planning his next move, Raphael had had a long time to think about what had gone wrong. 'So meticulously planned,' he told himself and he was furious, wallowing in his failure and looking for someone to blame: he vented his anger on Constantin. The fact that he had been drunk and in a careless moment had told Constantin of his secret about Madrigal, left no place for self-blame.

He had always been so sure of himself and his importance that he couldn't even contemplate that, once knowing of the illegal act, Constantin would not stand by him. He expected him to support him, to be loyal, and to collude with his terrible deception. After all, Constantin was his employee and he was shocked at his response.

"What!" Constantin had shouted. "You mean you had planned right from the beginning to sting and defraud? What about Antoinette and James? They have spent a fortune, not to mention hours of hard work and dedication to stage your exhibition. How could you do this?"

"Don't be so sentimental," Raphael replied scathingly. "I need the money badly. No-one will get hurt and, anyway, they are just two unimportant people unknowingly helping me out of a financial crisis."

Constantin could not believe what he was hearing. "But you tell everyone about how wealthy and famous you are."

"I have my reputation to maintain. People are so gullible, believing everything you tell them, even you! My money has gone, so I had to find a way of raising more. I insisted on a very high insurance premium for Madrigal. Stolen, and then disappearing, means I can claim the ten million pounds insurance on it."

Appalled, Constantin continued. "I have been a dupe too. Do you have no scruples? I don't believe you do."

"Well, whether you like it or not, Mr Patras, you are implicated are you not? People would never believe you didn't know what was happening, so you had better keep quiet. I employ you and, as your employer, I forbid you to say anything."

"Forbid! Who the hell do you think you are? Well, I cannot be party to your scheme. You are an evil man and I won't be an accessory to your crime."

"Crime? It isn't a crime. It is my painting, I can do what I want with it."

"I can't believe I'm hearing this."

"Well, you can hear this and clearly too. You are no longer employed. I'm sacking you, so go now and don't try to come to the opening at the gallery tomorrow."

"Good," Constantin replied. "I couldn't contemplate ever working for you again."

"You'll regret it." Raphael spat the words at him. "And I'm warning you, if you try to do anything or tell anyone about the theft, I will deny everything and blame it on you. You will not be safe from me!"

"Are you threatening me? You won't get away with this, Raphael."

"Who says? Go on, just go, you aren't even worth talking to." He turned his back on Constantin who left rapidly, not quite knowing what to do. He checked out of the hotel and Raphael didn't see him again. But he wondered what Constantin would do, fearing that he would foil his plans if he could. Yet, with his arrogant and egocentric opinion of himself, he felt quite capable of preventing Constantin. Raphael underestimated everyone, he thought no-one was as clever as him and was supremely confident that no-one would figure out what he was up to.

Constantin, in the meantime, had much to think about. When Eleanor had texted him, he had told her that he was fine. But fine he wasn't, and he rang Eleanor to tell her he was upset about something Raphael had said. He couldn't, however, bring himself to give more details. "I'll catch up with you when I know more," he said.

Eleanor didn't know what to make of the conversation but hoped to find out more at the gallery next day.

Then, before Constantin could do anything constructive, the painting had disappeared. Knowing he couldn't foil the plot, he now had to consider what Raphael would do. Constantin was concerned that, if he went to the police, he would incriminate himself. He felt cowardly, yet he would do all he could not to let Raphael succeed in destroying Madrigal. By thinking back to the various events of the last few months, he remembered occasions when Raphael had acted even more strangely than usual. He had no time to waste. After all, Raphael had already stolen the painting, perhaps disposed of it too, but he thought not. He now understood why Madrigal was unframed and comprised light materials. Raphael needed to carry it, but to where and when? Then suddenly, he knew.

* * *

The theft was not as easy as Raphael had thought it would be. Madrigal was still bulky and heavy and he was forced to cut it up and roll it like carpet. He took so much longer than anticipated. He was panicked and exhausted but still managed eventually to carry the pieces out to a hired van outside La Perle. It was now too late to do much more. The island was waking up for the new day, so he parked the van close to the marina, risking that no-one would suspect, then returned to his hotel to calm down and wait until darkness.

But Constantin was ahead of Raphael. By lunchtime, he had walked to Ca'lou and was prepared to spend as long as it took until Raphael arrived. He was confident that this was where he would come; to him, there was no other explanation as to why he should have been obsessed by this tiny island. It was a horrible place but he concealed himself in the bunker and waited, hoping that he had guessed correctly and that this was Raphael's hiding place. There were better places to hide, thought Constantin. This was dark, cold, eerie, damp and very spooky, especially when – as dusk approached – he was overwhelmed as seemingly thousands of bats left their roosts, heading out to feed in the encroaching darkness. They flew around his head, eager for a night of hunting. This whole place disturbed him, and, if it hadn't been for the sounds of the sea, the whole cave-like structure would have been heavy and suffocating with its cold, dark silence. Then suddenly, he knew his hunch had been right.

* * *

Chartering a small cruiser under a false name, Raphael loaded Madrigal under cover of darkness. He was no sailor, but 'he would manage,' he told himself. Lugging the painting up the beach and into the bunker was no easy task either. 'It will be worth it,' he told himself. 'For ten million pounds insurance, of course it will.' Then, after a final effort, he was done. "This is it! Success!" Raphael laughed. He felt flushed with pride at how clever he was.

Keeping perfectly still, Constantin now realised that Raphael was going to burn the canvas. 'Quite clever,' he told himself, 'it would seem no more than many other campfire ashes left by locals on their bunker visits.'

Raphael realised the canvas would take some time to burn through. 'No matter, I've got all night,' he told himself. He searched his pockets for matches and was about to strike one.

"I wouldn't do that if I were you." Stunned, Raphael stopped. He knew immediately that it was Constantin. "When I thought about it, it was obvious you would come here to hide it. At the time, I just couldn't understand why you were so keen to see this place and why you were so furtive about it. You wouldn't normally go anywhere near such a grotty, dirty place. So, there had to be a good reason."

"Very clever of you," Raphael answered, his voice laced with sarcasm and hate. He couldn't see Constantin, but knew he wasn't far away, and he thought desperately for a way out of the situation.

"Throw down the matches and move away!" ordered Constantin. "Keep perfectly still. I've already contacted the police, and they're on their way. You can't get away with this, Raphael."

"I don't believe you. You weren't totally sure where I would be. There are no police on the way."

Constantin hadn't thought about his next move. Raphael was right, but he would do it now. He couldn't have imagined the danger he was in. Raphael was a desperate man. "Aren't they?" he answered. "Well, we'll find out. I'll ring them again; they will be very near by now." Then, when he took out his phone, Constantin realised his mistake, as its light immediately gave away his hiding place.

Raphael seized his opportunity, charging towards Constantin with the scissors he had used to cut up Madrigal. Unarmed and taken by surprise, Constantin had little chance even as he saw the threat and set off at a run. He tripped over debris on the bunker floor. Raphael saw his chance and stabbed him in the chest and stomach. Constantin tried to stand, but Raphael, taking no chances, rushed him, picked up a large stone and smashed it into the back of Constantin's head. He fell back and didn't get up again. Raphael knew he had killed him. Panicking, he watched as blood oozed out of the wound.

"Stupid, stupid man! He could have shared the money with me. I didn't want to kill him, but it's done now." He felt no remorse. Rather, he was angry with Constantin for complicating his plans.

'I must get rid of the body. I can't let him be found here, but what can I do?' Moving him was not easy. He was heavy, and Raphael dragged rather than lifted him. Finally, he got the body close to the gun emplacement, which was higher than he thought. Sweating and breathless, he struggled to lift the body up and only managed it by finding and standing on some stones for extra lift.

"Oh my God, this is terrible!" he cried. But finally he lifted Constantin's body onto the gun shelf and, with one final push, the body rolled along and dropped heavily into the sea. Raphael had blood on his clothes, felt nauseous and was shaking. He forced himself to be calm as he realised that he still needed to also dispose of Madrigal. He searched for the matches and set the canvas on fire, trying to keep the flames low and smouldering. When it seemed that everything was burned, he kicked over the hot ashes and headed as quickly as possible to the exit, roughly scuffing over footprints and other signs of disturbance with dust and debris from the floor. Once outside, he breathed deeply. The fresh air was welcome but the realisation of what he had done made him sick and he vomited into the rough island grass. The sky was lightening; he couldn't believe it had taken all night.

"Well, he brought it on himself," he said, feeling justified. "And now I've sorted it all, I can keep the money for myself."

He thought no more about it, concentrating instead on his escape. 'I'll make for Normandy,' he decided, 'the police won't think I've stayed so close by.'

* * *

So, holed up in Honfleur, he had time to reflect. How gullible people are. Those gallery owners – how naïve to believe it was in my interests to exhibit at their quaint little place, so provincial. Me, for my reputation, wealth… yes I'll do anything, whatever it takes for people to keep believing in me. I need to move on from here, though, get that insurance somehow. I'll ring and ask the broker to send a claim form to the studio. I'll deal with it when I get back to London. I'm not done yet, I'll find my way out, oh yes, and my success will continue. No regrets, only looking forward to the future, my future!

Epilogue

The whole affair had hit James and Antoinette hard. When all the facts had emerged they wondered whether they could weather the storm.

Raphael being in prison was a great vindication, especially for Constantin, but it had not helped their situation. They had lost a lot of money and no insurance would be forthcoming, even though they had paid for it. Yet, on a late autumn day, they felt able to reflect and had walked over to Ca'lou, and with the locked bunker behind them, looked across to Guernsey, the island they loved. There was a stiff breeze blowing off the sea, scattering sand into their faces and whistling as the wind blew in circles around the bunker, with waves lashing against the sturdy concrete walls. They headed to the monastery ruins, a more sheltered spot, where they sat close together on one of the monastery walls. The wind still whirled around them and for a few minutes both were lost in their own thoughts.

"So that's why he sulked," said Antoinette, her words muffled as they were carried away on the wind.

"Sorry, Annie, I didn't hear what you said."

"I was thinking about the day I brought Raphael here, He said he was captivated by the island and wanted to have a look round. We searched all the nooks and crannies and he suddenly went into a big sulk. Of course, we now know how temperamental he could be, but at the tine I just couldn't understand what was wrong."

"But you do now?"

"Yes. I'm sure he was looking for somewhere to hide Madrigal but was frustrated and angry when he couldn't find anywhere. So he sulked, wanted to get back across the causeway and didn't speak all the way back. Obviously, he came back here later and decided to use the bunker instead.

Everything he did in Guernsey was part of his plan. I feel sick when I think how he manipulated us."

"We were both totally expendable, weren't we?" James admitted.

"Both we and our gallery were simply convenient for his plans. It's really sickening; it's hard to accept or even understand that there are such unscrupulous people."

"You're right, you read about such people but don't really think they could invade your own life."

Antoinette continued. "It's incredible when you think about the planning that went into the scam and his audacity and confidence to carry it out. Even down to Madrigal itself. He planned all along for it not to be a large, framed painting. He knew that it would be too large to handle on his own. But, creating it as he did, he could just roll it up and carry it away. Were we really so naïve, James?"

"No, he was very clever. Maybe we were a little gullible, but remember we weren't the first people to fall for his fraud."

"That's true – it's hard to understand why no-one found him out before. Why didn't someone check his credentials with the art college and things?"

"In retrospect," James continued, "it seems obvious, but he was so plausible and we didn't check either. He probably should have been an actor – he can certainly play a part!"

"It wasn't a part when he killed Constantin, though, was it? It showed his real evil self." Antoinette shivered as she recalled the horror. "We're certainly lucky to have survived, maybe not unscathed, but we can still fight another day. What of our reputation though, James, can we ever recover it?"

James replied confidently, whether or not he really felt it. "Of course we can. Mum was right when she said that people have short memories. We will soon be yesterday's news."

"I hope you're right. Come on, James let's walk back, I'm feeling cold." They set off together back to the causeway. "You know, if we only ever sell souvenirs of Guernsey in future, I won't mind. I will be happy. I love you and that's all that really matters. And together we can put our lovely gallery back on track."

"Yes we can, and I love you too and always will." They exchanged a loving kiss.

"Just one more thing though, Annie."

"What's that?"

"Don't answer the phone again to anyone else who claims to be a rich and famous artist!"

"You," said Antoinette with a smile and punched him lightly in the arm.

* * *

At the same time, in the Guernsey newspaper offices, Daniel was putting the finishing touches to an article. The elation he'd felt being involved in a murder investigation had receded and he was finding it hard to focus again on the mundane events of a small island. He looked forward eagerly to the possibility of another exciting event, but he knew it was something that didn't happen often in Guernsey. But still, he could hope. He had continued to think too of Tanya, but she obviously didn't want to keep in touch. Then his phone rang.

"Hello, Daniel West, news desk. Can I help you?"

"Hi Daniel," said a familiar voice. "I've looked at your slip of paper for weeks now, and I've finally plucked up the courage to ring you."

"Oh, Tanya, I am so glad you did. His heart missed a beat.

But that is another story!

You may also enjoy...

The Jonquil

Marilyn Parkes-Seddon

Also from Marilyn Parkes-Seddon

Seeking the Scallop Shell

Marilyn Parkes-Seddon

with foreword by the Dean of Carlisle Cathedral
the Very Revd Mark Boyling